QUEEN'S BUREAU OF INVESTIGATION

Queen's Bureau of Investigation

by ELLERY QUEEN

Little, Brown and Company
Boston · Toronto

MYSTERY

Published simultaneously in Canada
by Little, Brown & Company (Canada) Limited

PRINTED IN THE UNITED STATES OF AMERICA

Memo

Hᴇʀᴇ ᴀɴᴅ ᴛʜᴇʀᴇ in the closed-case records of Queen's Bureau of Investigation will be found a file marked *Special*. Such files contain records of cases that turned up something of peculiar interest—in one an unusual clue, perhaps, in others a memorable criminal or a surprising situation.

Many of these cases went through the main office divisions of Q.B.I., such as the departments specializing in Murder, Holdup, Blackmail, Narcotics, Racket, Kidnaping, and the like. But some, of rarer types, were assigned to appropriate subdivisions of the Bureau—for example, the Dying Message Dept., the Buried Treasure Dept., the Magic Dept. and, of course, the closely guarded top-floor office of the Impossible Crime Dept.

Here are eighteen such adventures in investigation.

Ellery Queen

Directory

Queen's Bureau of Investigation

BLACKMAIL DEPT.

Money Talks

Blackmail speaks its own peculiar dialect, but it has this advantage over other forms of expression: It is the universal language, understood by all.

Including the Sicilian. Mrs. Alfredo had heard its hissed accents, and she wept.

Ellery thought he had never seen a less likely victim. Mrs. Alfredo was as broad as a *gnocco,* her skin had a time-grated Parmesan look, and her hands had been marinated in the Chianti of hard work. It seemed that she ran a very modest boarding-house in the West Fifties which sagged under a mortgage. How, then, blackmail?

But then he heard about Mrs. Alfredo's daughter Lucia, and Lucia's Tosca, and how encouraging the Metropolitan Opera people had been about Lucia's *"Vissi d'arte, vissi d'amore,"* and Ellery thought he detected the sibilant accent, too.

Lucia's career was in jeopardy.

"On what ground, Mrs. Alfredo?" he asked.

The ground was foreign. In her youth Mrs. Alfredo had been a cook. One summer an employer had taken her to England, in England she had met an Englishman, and the Englishman had married her. Perfidious Albion! Within a month Alfred had vanished with her life's savings. What was worse, although eventually she recovered most of her money, the glamorous Alfred was discovered to possess another wife who claimed, and proved, priority. And what was worst, in inexorable course the poor woman found herself about to have Alfred's baby. Mrs. Alfredo, as she had begun to call herself, fled Bloomsbury for her adopted land, posing as a widow and never telling anyone except Lucia her bigamous secret; and in the prehistoric days when a house could be bought with the widow's mite she had purchased the ancient property in the West Fifties which was now her livelihood and the hope of Lucia's operatic career.

"Long time I scare that Lucia's secret come out," she wept to Ellery, "but then a friend from Bloomsbury write me that Alfred die, so Lucia and I forget our shame. Until now, *signore*. Now it comes out. If I do not pay the money."

The crudely lettered note had been pushed under her bedroom door. Five thousand dollars was demanded for silence about her daughter's illegal state. "How do they know, *Signor* Queen? Never do we tell anyone—never!" The money was to be placed under the loose newel post on the second-floor landing of her house.

"A boarder," said Ellery grimly. "How many boarders do you have, Mrs. Alfredo?"

"Three. Mist' Collins, Mist'—"

"Do you have five thousand dollars, Mrs. Alfredo?"

"Sì. I do not pay off the mortgage—I save for Lucia's Voice Lesson. But if now I pay this money, Maestro Zaggiore give no more lesson! And if I do not pay, it will be known about me, about Lucia. It break Lucia's heart, *signore*. Ruin her career. Already she is cry and cry over this."

"Young hearts take a heap of breaking and careers with real talent behind them don't ruin easily. Take my advice, Mrs. Alfredo: Don't pay."

"No," agreed Mrs. Alfredo with a certain cunning. " 'Cause you catch him quick, hey?"

The next morning Mrs. Alfredo's newest boarder awakened in one of her feather beds to an enchantment. "*Un bel dì,*" sang Cho-Cho-San, "*vedremo levarsi un fil di fumo. . . .*" The piano sounded as if it had served aboard the U.S. Gunboat *Abraham Lincoln* along with Lieutenant Pinkerton, but the voice coming through the aged walls rang as sweet and rich as a newly minted coin. And Ellery rose, and dressed like a struggling writer just in from Kansas City, and went downstairs to Mrs. Alfredo's dining room determined that Lucia should have her chance.

At breakfast he met Lucia, who was beautiful, and the three boarders, who were not. Mr. Arnold was small, thin, pedantic, and looked like a clerk in a secondhand bookshop, which was exactly what he was; Mr. Bordelaux was medium-sized, fat, garrulous, and looked like a French wine salesman, which was exactly what *he* was; and Mr. Collins was large, powerful, and slangy and if he had not turned out to be a taxicab driver Ellery would have turned in his honorary police badge. They were all three amiable, they took turns ogling Lucia and praising Mrs. Alfredo's *uovo con peperoni*, and they departed—Mr. Arnold for his Cooper Square bookshop, Mr. Bordelaux for his vinous rounds, and Mr. Collins for his battered taxi—in a perfect corona of innocence.

The next three days were incidental. Ellery ransacked Mr. Arnold's room and Mr. Bordelaux's room and Mr. Collins's room. In the evenings and in the mornings he studied his ABCs, as he privately called the three boarders, discussing books with Mr. Arnold, wines with Mr. Bordelaux, and nags and dames with Mr. Collins. He tried to reassure Lucia, who was tragically desperate. He tried to get Mrs. Alfredo's permission to take the note and her story to the police, for their assistance along certain lines he had in mind; Mrs. Alfredo became hysterical. He advised her to deliver a note to the loose newel post saying that it would take a few days to raise the money. This she consented to do, and Ellery carefully refrained from insomnia that night, merely making sure that entry from outside the building would leave traces. And in the morning the note was gone and there were no traces. . . . Ellery did all the things one does in such cases, and what he gathered for his pains was the knowledge that the blackmailer was Mr. Arnold the book clerk, or Mr. Bordelaux the wine drummer, or Mr. Collins the taxi driver, and he had known that from the beginning.

But the fourth morning dawned with a bang. The emotional hand of Mrs. Alfredo was on his bedroom door, and its owner cried doom.

"My Lucia! She lock herself in her room! She does not answer! She is at least dead!"

Ellery soothed the frantic woman and hurried into the hall. From three doorways three heads protruded.

"Something wrong?" exclaimed Mr. Arnold.

"Is it that there is a fire?" cried Mr. Bordelaux.

"What gives?" growled Mr. Collins.

Ellery tried Lucia's door. It was latched from inside. He knocked. No answer. He listened. He heard nothing.

"Dr. Santelli!" moaned Mrs. Alfredo. "I get *il dottore!*"

"Do that," said Ellery. "Collins, help me break this door in."

"Lemme at it," said the powerful Mr. Collins.

But the old door was like iron.

"The ax of the fire," howled Mr. Bordelaux; and he flew down the stairs after Mrs. Alfredo, carpet slippers flapping.

"Here," panted Mr. Arnold, appearing with a chair. "Let's have a look through that fanlight." He scrambled onto the chair and peered through the transom above the door. "She's on the bed. She's been sick—She's just lying there—"

"Any blood, Arnold?" asked Ellery anxiously.

"No. . . . But there's a box of sweets. And a tin of something—"

"Oh, no," groaned Ellery. "Can you make out the label?"

Mr. Arnold's Adam's crabapple bobbed before the little rectangular window above the door. "It looks like . . . rat poison."

At which Mr. Bordelaux appeared with the fire ax and Mrs. Alfredo with an excited gentleman in his undershirt who looked like Arturo Toscanini. They all tumbled in to find that Lucia had attempted to commit suicide by filling some chocolates with rat poison and bravely swallowing them.

"*Molto, molto,*" said Dr. Santelli. "Her tummy rejects. All to go out!" And later, the doctor called Mrs. Alfredo and Ellery in, and he said, "Lucia. *Cara.* Open the eye."

"Mama," quavered Lucia.

"'*Bina,*" wept Mama.

But Ellery set Mama firmly to one side. "Lucia, the Met needs you—believe me! You're never to do such a foolish thing again. Anyway, you won't have to, because now I know which one of Mama's boarders has been trying to blackmail her, and I think I can assure you that he won't try it again."

And later Ellery said to the silent man holding the suitcase, "My clients will press no charge so long as you're smart enough to keep their secret. I might add, before you go, that you're far too careless to make a successful blackmailer."

"Careless?" said the man with the suitcase, sullenly.

"Oh, criminally. Mrs. Alfredo and Lucia never have told anyone about the illegal union. So the blackmailer must have learned about it from the bigamist himself. But since Alfred was an Englishman who lived—and died—in England, the great likelihood was that the blackmailer was English, too, you see.

"You've tried hard to conceal it, but in the excitement of this morning's events you slipped. Only an Englishman would have called a rectangular transom a 'fanlight,' chocolates 'sweets,' and a can of poison a 'tin.' So if you're ever tempted to stray from your bookselling to try a scoundrelly stunt like this again—watch your language, Mr. Arnold!"

FIX DEPT.

A Matter of Seconds

You DON'T HAVE to be a fight expert to recall what happened in the ring that wild night the Champ fought Billy (the Kid) Bolo. Fans are still talking about how it put Wickiup, Colorado, on the map. But the odds are you've never heard how close that fight came to not being fought.

You remember how Wickiup got the match in the first place. The deputation from the Wickiup Chamber of Commerce, headed by millionaire cattleman Sam Pugh, trooped into the promoter's New York office, plunked down a seating plan of the new Wickiup Natural Amphitheater—capacity 75,-

000—and a satchel containing a guarantee of $250,000 cash money, and flew back home with a contract for what turned out to be—figuring the TV, radio, and movie take—the first million-dollar gate west of Chicago in the history of boxing.

It promised to be a real whingding, too, well worth any sport's investment. Both fighters were rough, tough and indestructible, their orthodox style carrying no surprises except in the sudden-death department. Anything could happen from a one-round knockout to a hospital bed for two.

The Champ trained at the Wickiup Country Club and Billy the Kid at the big Pugh ranch, and days before the fight every hotel, motel, trailer camp and tepee within three hundred miles was hanging out the *No Vacancy* sign. Wickiup became the Eldorado of every fight fan, sportswriter, gambler and grifter between Key West and Puget Sound who could scare up a grubstake.

Ellery was in Wickiup to see the contest as the guest of old Sam Pugh, who owed him something for a reason that's another story.

The fight was scheduled for 8 p.m. Mountain Time, to make the 10 p.m. TV date for the Eastern fans. Ellery first heard that something was wrong exactly an hour and a half before ringtime.

He was hanging around the Comanche Bar of the Redman Hotel, waiting for his host to pick him up for the drive out to the Amphitheater, when he was paged by a bellboy.

"Mr. Queen? Mr. Pugh wants you to come up to Suite 101. Urgent."

The cattleman himself answered Ellery's knock. His purple-sage complexion looked moldy. "Come in, son!"

In the suite Ellery found the State Boxing Commissioner,

nine leading citizens of Wickiup, and Tootsie Cogan, Billy the Kid's bald little manager. Tootsie was crying, and the other gentlemen looked half inclined to join him.

"What's the matter?" asked Ellery.

"The Kid," growled Sam Pugh, "has been kidnaped."

"Snatched," wept Cogan. "At three o'clock I feed him a rare steak at Mr. Pugh's ranch and I make him lay down for a snooze. I run over for a last-minute yak with Chick Kraus, the Champ's manager, about the rules, and while I'm gone—"

"Four masked men with guns snatched the Kid," said the cattleman. "We've been negotiating with them by phone ever since. They want a hundred thousand dollars' ransom."

"Or no fight," snarled the Boxing Commissioner. "Eastern gangsters!"

"It'll ruin us," groaned one of the local elite. "The businessmen of this town put up a quarter of a million guarantee. Not to mention the lawsuits—"

"I think I get the picture, gentlemen," said Ellery. "With the fight less than ninety minutes off, there's no time to climb a high horse. I take it you're paying?"

"We've managed to raise the cash among us," said the old cattleman, nodding toward a bloated briefcase on the table, "and, Ellery, we've told 'em that you're going to deliver it. Will you?"

"You know I will, Sam," said Ellery. "Maybe I can get a line on them at the same time—"

"No, you'll put the whammy on it!" shrieked the Kid's manager. "Just get my boy back, in shape to climb in that ring!"

"You couldn't, anyway. They're not showing their dirty faces," rasped Sam Pugh. "They've named a neutral party, too, and he's agreed to act for them."

"What you might call a matter of seconds, eh? Who is he, Sam?"

"Know Sime Jackman, the newspaperman?"

"The dean of West Coast sportswriters? By reputation only; it's tops. Maybe if Jackman and I work together—"

"Sime's had to promise he'd keep his mouth shut," said the Boxing Commissioner, "and in the forty years I've known him, damn it, he's never broken his word. Forget the sleuthing, Mr. Queen. Just see that Billy Bolo gets back in time."

"All right," sighed Ellery. "Sam, what can I do?"

"At seven o'clock sharp," said the cattleman, "you're to be in Sime Jackman's room at the Western Hotel—Room 442. Jackman will then notify the kidnapers some way that you're there with the ransom, and Billy Bolo will be released. They've promised that the Kid will walk into this room by seven-fifteen, unharmed and ready to climb into the ring, if we keep our word."

"How do you know they'll keep theirs?"

"You're not to leave the money with Jackman till I phone you, in his room, that the Kid's back safe."

"Then you'd better give me a password, Sam—voices can be imitated. In my ear . . . if you gentlemen don't mind?"

A stocky man with white hair and keen blue eyes opened the door of Room 442 in the Western Hotel at Ellery's rap.

"You're Queen, I take it. Come on in. I'm Sime Jackman."

Ellery looked around while the newspaperman shut the door. On the telephone table stood a battered portable typewriter and a bottle of Scotch. There was no one else in the room.

"I think," said Ellery, "I'd like some identification."

The whitehaired man stared. Then he grinned and fished in his pockets. "Driver's license—press card—you'll find my name engraved on the back of this presentation watch from the National Sportswriters' Association—"

"I'm sold." Ellery opened the briefcase and dumped its contents on the bed. The money was in $1,000 bundles, marked on the bank wrappers—tens, twenties, and fifties. "Are you going to take the time to count it?"

"Hell, no. I want to see that fight tonight!" The sportswriter went to the window.

"I was told you'd immediately notify the kidnapers—"

"That's what I'm doing." Jackman raised and lowered the windowshade rapidly several times. "You don't think those lice gave me any phone numbers, do you? This is the signal I was told to give—they must have a man watching my window. I suppose he'll phone them it's okay. Well, that's that."

"Have you actually seen any of them?" Ellery asked.

"Have a heart, Queen," grinned the newspaperman. "I gave my word I wouldn't answer any questions. Well, now all we can do is wait for Sam Pugh's phone call. How about a drink?"

"I'll take a raincheck." Ellery sat down on the bed beside the ransom money. "What's the *modus operandi*, Jackman? How do you get the money to them?"

But the whitehaired man merely poured himself a drink. "Ought to be a pretty good scrap," he murmured.

"You win," said Ellery ruefully. "Yes, it should. How do you rate Bolo's chances? After all this, his nerves will be shot higher than Pike's Peak."

"The Kid? He was born without any. And when he gets mad, the way he must be right now—"

"Then you think he's got a chance to take the Champ?"

"If those punks didn't sap him, I make it the Kid by a K.O."

"You're the expert. You figure he's got the punch to put a bull like the Champ away?"

"Did you see the Kid's last fight?" smiled the sportswriter. "Artie Starr's nobody's setup. Yet Bolo hit him three right hooks so fast and murderous the second and third exploded on Starr's chin while he was still on his way to the canvas. It took his handlers ten minutes to bring him to—"

The phone made them both jump.

"They must have had the Kid around the corner!" Ellery said.

"You better answer it."

Ellery raced to the phone. "Queen speaking. Who is this?"

"It's me—Sam!" roared Sam Pugh's voice. "Listen, son—"

"Hold it. What's the password?"

"Oh! Solar plexus." Ellery nodded, relieved. "The Kid's back, Ellery," the cattleman exulted, "and he's all riled up and r'arin' to go. Release the money. See you at ringside!" His phone clicked.

"Okay?" smiled the whitehaired man.

"Yes," Ellery smiled back, "so now I can let you have it." And, swinging the telephone receiver, Ellery clubbed him neatly above the left ear. He was over at the clothes closet yanking the door open even before the whitehaired man bounced on the carpet. "So it *was* the closet he parked you in," Ellery said cheerfully to the trussed, gagged figure on the closet floor. "Well, we'll have you out of these ropes in a jiffy, Mr. Jackman, and then we'll settle the hash of this doublecrossing road agent!"

While the real Sime Jackman stood guard over the prostrate man, Ellery stuffed the money back into the briefcase. "Hijacker?" asked the newspaperman without rancor.

"No, indeed," said Ellery. "He couldn't have been a hijacker, because the gang released the Kid after this man gave the signal. So I knew he was one of them. When they told you I was to be the contact man, you said something about you and me not knowing each other, didn't you? I thought so. That's what gave this operator his big idea. He'd put you on ice, and when I handed him the ransom thinking he was you, he'd run out on his pals."

"But how," demanded the sportswriter, "did you know he wasn't me?"

"He said in the Bolo-Starr fight the Kid flattened Starr with three right hooks. You could hardly have become the dean of West Coast sportswriters and a national fight expert, Jackman, without learning that in the lexicon of boxing there's no such blow as a right hook for a fighter with the orthodox stance. The righthand equivalent of a left hook in a righthanded fighter is a right cross."

"Why, the palooka," scowled the newspaperman, taking a fresh grip on the unconscious gangster's gun as the man stirred. "But about this ransom, Queen. I don't know what to do. After all, the rest of the gang did keep their word and return the Kid. Do I keep mine and deliver the dough to them, or does this bum's doublecross take me off the hook?"

"Hm. Nice problem in ethics." Ellery glanced at his watch and frowned. "We'll miss the fight unless we hurry! Tell you what, Sime."

"What?"

"We'll pass the buck—or should I say bucks?—to a higher authority." Ellery grinned and picked up the bruised phone. "Desk? Two reliable cops for immediate guard duty, please, and meanwhile get me the nearest office of the FBI—rush!"

IMPOSSIBLE CRIME DEPT.

The Three Widows

To THE NORMAL PALATE the taste of murder is unpleasant. But Ellery is an epicure in these matters and certain of his cases, he deposes, possess a flavor which lingers on the tongue. Among these dangerous delicacies he places high the Case of the Three Widows.

Two of the widows were sisters: Penelope, to whom money was nothing, and Lyra, to whom it was everything, consequently each required large amounts of it. Both having buried thriftless husbands at an early age, they returned to the Murray Hill manse of their father with what everyone suspected was relief, for old Theodore Hood was generously provided with the coin of the republic and he had always been indulgent with his daughters. Shortly after Penelope and Lyra repossessed their maiden beds, however, Theodore Hood took a second wife, a cathedral-like lady of great force of character. Alarmed, the sisters gave battle, which their stepmother grimly joined. Old Theodore, caught in their crossfire, yearned only for peace. Eventually he found it, leaving a household inhabited by widows exclusively.

One evening not long after their father's death Penelope the plump and Lyra the lean were summoned by a servant to the drawing room of the Hood pile. They found waiting for them Mr. Strake, the family lawyer.

Mr. Strake's commonest utterance fell like a sentence from the lips of a judge; but tonight, when he pronounced "Will you be seated, ladies," his tone was so ominous that the crime was obviously a hanging one. The ladies exchanged glances and declined.

In a few moments the tall doors squealed into the Victorian walls and Sarah Hood came in feebly on the arm of Dr. Benedict, the family physician.

Mrs. Hood surveyed her stepdaughters with a sort of contempt, her head teetering a little. Then she said, "Dr. Benedict and Mr. Strake will speak their pieces, then I'll speak mine."

"Last week," began Dr. Benedict, "your stepmother came to my office for her semiannual checkup. I gave her the usual thorough examination. Considering her age, I found her in extraordinarily good health. Yet the very next day she came down sick—for the first time, by the way, in eight years. I thought then that she'd picked up an intestinal virus, but Mrs. Hood made a rather different diagnosis. I considered it fantastic.

However, she insisted that I make certain tests. I did, and she was right. She had been poisoned."

The plump cheeks of Penelope went slowly pink, and the lean cheeks of Lyra went slowly pale.

"I feel sure," Dr. Benedict went on, addressing a point precisely midway between the sisters, "that you'll understand why I must warn you that from now on I shall examine your stepmother every day."

"Mr. Strake," said old Mrs. Hood, smiling.

"Under your father's will," said Mr. Strake abruptly, also addressing the equidistant point, "each of you receives a small allowance from the income of the estate. The bulk of that income goes to your stepmother for as long as she shall live. But at Mrs. Hood's demise, you inherit the principal of some two million dollars, in equal shares. In other words, you two are the only persons in the world who will benefit by your stepmother's death. As I've informed both Mrs. Hood and Dr. Benedict—if you are not warned by your extremely good fortune in failing in this dastardly murder attempt, I shall devote what remains of my life to seeing that you are punished to the full extent of the law. In fact, it was my advice to call in the police immediately."

"Call them now!" cried Penelope.

Lyra said nothing.

"I could call them now, Penny," said Mrs. Hood with the same faint smile, "but you're both very clever and it might not settle anything. My strongest protection would be to throw the two of you out of this house; unfortunately, your father's will prevents me. Oh, I understand your impatience to be rid of me. You have luxurious tastes which aren't satisfied by my simple way of living. You'd both like to remarry, and with the money you could buy yourselves second husbands." The old lady leaned forward a little. "But I have bad news for you. My mother died at ninety-nine, my father at a hundred and three. Dr. Benedict tells me I can live another thirty years, and I have every intention of doing so." She struggled to her feet, still smiling. "In fact, I'm taking certain precautions to make sure of it," she said; and she went out.

Exactly one week later Ellery was seated beside Mrs. Hood's great mahogany fourposter, under the anxious eyes of Dr. Benedict and Mr. Strake.

She had been poisoned again. Fortunately, Dr. Benedict had caught it in time.

Ellery bent over the old lady's face, which looked more like plaster than flesh. "These precautions of yours, Mrs. Hood—"

"I tell you," she whispered, "it was impossible."

"Still," said Ellery cheerfully, "it was done. So let's resume. You had your bedroom windows barred and a new lock installed on that door, the single key to which you've kept on your person at all times. You've bought your own food. You've done your own cooking in this room and you've eaten here alone. Clearly, then, the poison could not have been introduced into your food before, during, or after its preparation. Further, you tell me you purchased new dishes, have kept them here, and you and you alone have been handling them. Consequently the poison couldn't have been put on or in the cooking utensils, china, glassware, or cutlery involved in your meals. How then was the poison administered?"

"That's the problem," cried Dr. Benedict.

"A problem, Mr. Queen," muttered Mr. Strake, "that I

thought—and Dr. Benedict agreed—was more your sort of thing than the police's."

"Well, my sort of thing is always simple," replied Ellery, "provided you see it. Mrs. Hood, I'm going to ask you a great many questions. Is it all right, Doctor?"

Dr. Benedict felt the old lady's pulse, and he nodded. Ellery began. She replied in whispers, but with great positiveness. She had bought a new toothbrush and fresh tooth paste for her siege. Her teeth were still her own. She had an aversion to medication and took no drugs or palliatives of any kind. She drank nothing but water. She did not smoke, eat sweets, chew gum, use cosmetics. . . . The questions went on and on. Ellery asked every one he could think of, and then he shook up his brain to think of more.

Finally, he thanked Mrs. Hood, patted her hand, and went out with Dr. Benedict and Mr. Strake.

"What's your diagnosis, Mr. Queen?" asked Dr. Benedict.

"Your verdict," said Mr. Strake impatiently.

"Gentlemen," said Ellery, "when I eliminated her drinking water by examining the pipes and faucets in her bathroom and finding they hadn't been tampered with, I'd ruled out the last possibility."

"And yet it's being administered orally," snapped Dr. Benedict. "That's my finding and I've been careful to get medical corroboration."

"If that is a fact, Doctor," said Ellery, "then there is only one remaining explanation."

"What's that?"

"Mrs. Hood is poisoning herself. If I were you I would call in a psychiatrist. Good day!"

*   *   *

Ten days later Ellery was back in Sarah Hood's bedroom. The old lady was dead. She had succumbed to a third poisoning attack.

On being notified, Ellery had promptly said to his father, Inspector Queen, "Suicide."

But it was not suicide. The most painstaking investigation by police experts, utilizing all the resources of criminological science, failed to turn up a trace of the poison, or of a poison container or other possible source, in Mrs. Hood's bedroom or bath. Scoffing, Ellery went over the premises himself. His smile vanished. He found nothing to contradict either the old lady's previous testimony or the findings of the experts. He grilled the servants. He examined with remorseless efficiency Penelope, who kept weeping, and Lyra, who kept snarling. Finally, he left.

It was the kind of problem which Ellery's thinking apparatus, against all the protests of his body, cannot let alone. For forty-six hours he lived in his own head, fasting and sleepless, ceaselessly pacing the treadmill of the Queen apartment floor. In the forty-seventh hour Inspector Queen took him forcibly by the arm and put him to bed.

"I thought so," said the Inspector. "Over a hundred and one. What hurts, son?"

"My whole existence," mumbled Ellery; and he submitted to aspirins, an ice bag, and a rare steak broiled in butter.

In the middle of the steak he shouted like a madman and clawed at the telephone.

"Mr. Strake? Ellery Queen! Meet me at the Hood house immediately!—yes, notify Dr. Benedict!—yes, now I know how Mrs. Hood was poisoned!"

And when they were gathered in the cavern of the Hood drawing room Ellery peered at plump Penelope and lean Lyra and he croaked, "Which one of you is intending to marry Dr. Benedict?"

And then he said, "Oh, yes, it has to be that. Only Penelope and Lyra benefit from their stepmother's murder, yet the only person who could physically have committed the murder is Dr. Benedict. . . . Did you ask how, Doctor?" asked Ellery courteously. "Why, very simply. Mrs. Hood experienced her first poisoning attack the day after her semiannual medical checkup—by you, Doctor. And thereafter, you announced, *you would examine Mrs. Hood every day.* There is a classic preliminary to every physician's examination of a patient. I submit, Dr. Benedict," said Ellery with a smile, "that you introduced the poison into Mrs. Hood's mouth on the same thermometer with which you took her temperature!"

RARE BOOK DEPT.

"My Queer Dean!"

The QUEERNESS OF Matthew Arnold Hope, beloved teacher of Ellery's Harvard youth and lately dean of liberal arts in a New York university, is legendary.

The story is told, for instance, of baffled students taking Dr. Hope's Shakespeare course for the first time. "History advises us that Richard II died peacefully at Pontefract, probably of pneumonia," Dr. Hope scolds. "But what does Shakespeare say, Act V, Scene V? That Exton struck him down," and here the famous authority on Elizabethan literature will pause for emphasis, "with a blushing crow!"

Imaginative sophomores have been known to suffer night-mare as a result of this remark. Older heads nod intelligently, of course, knowing that Dr. Hope meant merely to say—in fact, thought he was saying—"a crushing blow."

The good dean's unconscious spoonerisms, like the sayings of Miss Parker and Mr. Goldwyn, are reverently preserved by aficionados, among whom Ellery counts himself a charter member. It is Ellery who has saved for posterity that deathless pronouncement of Dr. Hope's to a freshman class in English composition: "All those who persist in befouling their theme papers with cant and other low expressions not in good usage are warned for the last time: Refine your style or be exiled from this course with the rest of the vanished Bulgarians!"

But perhaps Dean Hope's greatest exploit began recently in the faculty lunchroom. Ellery arrived at the dean's invitation to find him waiting impatiently at one of the big round tables with three members of the English Department.

"Dr. Agnes Lovell, Professor Oswald Gorman, Mr. Morgan Naseby," the dean said rapidly. "Sit down, Ellery. Mr. Queen will have the cute frocktail and the horned beef cash—only safe edibles on the menu today, my boy—well, go fetch, young man! Are you dreaming that you're back in class?" The waiter, a harried-looking freshman, fled. Then Dr. Hope said solemnly, "My friends, prepare for a surprise."

Dr. Lovell, a very large woman in a tight suit, said roguishly: "Wait, Matthew! Let me guess. Romance?"

"And who'd marry—in Macaulay's imperishable phrase—a living concordance?" said Professor Gorman in a voice like an abandoned winch. He was a tall freckled man with strawberry eyebrows and a quarrelsome jaw. "A real surprise, Dr. Hope, would be a departmental salary rise."

"A consummation devoutly et cetera," said Mr. Naseby, immediately blushing. He was a stout young man with an eager manner, evidently a junior in the department.

"May I have your attention?" Dean Hope looked about cautiously. "Suppose I tell you," he said in a trembling voice, "that by tonight I may have it within my power to deliver the death blow—I repeat, the death blow!—to the cockypop that Francis Bacon wrote Shakespeare's plays?"

There were two gasps, a snort, and one inquiring hum.

"Matthew!" squealed Dr. Lovell. "You'd be famous!"

"Immortal, Dean Hope," said Mr. Naseby adoringly.

"Deluded," said Professor Gorman, the snorter. "The Baconian benightedness, like the Marlowe mania, has no known specific."

"Ah, but even a fanatic," cried the dean, "would have to yield before the nature of this evidence."

"Sounds exciting, Doc," murmured Ellery. "What is it?"

"A man called at my office this morning, Ellery. He produced credentials identifying him as a London rare book dealer, Alfred Mimms. He has in his possession, he said, a copy of the 1613 edition of *The Essaies of Sir Francis Bacon Knight the kings solliciter generall*, an item ordinarily bringing four or five hundred dollars. He claims that this copy, however, is unique, *being inscribed on the title page in Bacon's own hand to Will Shakespeare.*"

Amid the cries, Ellery asked: "Inscribed how?"

"In an encomium," quavered Dean Hope, "an encomium to Shakespeare expressing Bacon's admiration and praise for—and I quote—'*the most excellent plaies of your sweet wit and hand*'!"

"Take that!" whispered Mr. Naseby to an invisible Baconian.

"That does it," breathed Dr. Lovell.

"That would do it," said Professor Gorman, "if."

"Did you actually see the book, Doc?" asked Ellery.

"He showed me a photostat of the title page. He'll have the original for my inspection tonight, in my office."

"And Mimms's asking price is—?"

"Ten thousand dollars."

"Proof positive that it's a forgery," said Professor Gorman rustily. "It's far too little."

"Oswald," hissed Dr. Lovell, "you creak, do you know that?"

"No, Gorman is right," said Dr. Hope. "An absurd price if the inscription is genuine, as I pointed out to Mimms. However, he had an explanation. He is acting, he said, at the instructions of the book's owner, a tax-poor British nobleman whose identity he will reveal tonight if I purchase the book. The owner, who has just found it in a castle room boarded up and forgotten for two centuries, prefers an American buyer in a confidential sale—for tax reasons, Mimms hinted. But, as a cultivated man, the owner wishes a scholar to have it rather than some ignorant Croesus. Hence the relatively low price."

"Lovely," glowed Mr. Naseby. "And so typically British."

"Isn't it," said Professor Gorman. "Terms cash, no doubt? On the line? Tonight?"

"Well, yes." The old dean took a bulging envelope from his breast pocket and eyed it ruefully. Then, with a sigh, he tucked it back. "Very nearly my life's savings . . . But I'm not altogether senile," Dr. Hope grinned. "I'm asking you to be present, Ellery—with Inspector Queen. I shall be working at my desk on administrative things into the evening. Mimms is due at eight o'clock."

"We'll be here at seven-thirty," promised Ellery. "By the way, Doc, that's a lot of money to be carrying around in your pocket. Have you confided this business to anyone else?"

"No, no."

"Don't. And may I suggest that you wait behind a locked door? Don't admit Mimms—or anyone else you don't trust— until we get here. I'm afraid, Doc, I share the professor's skepticism."

"Oh, so do I," murmured the dean. "The odds on this being a swindle are, I should think, several thousand to one. But one can't help saying to oneself . . . suppose it's not?"

It was nearly half-past seven when the Queens entered the Arts Building. Some windows on the upper floors were lit up where a few evening classes were in session, and the dean's office was bright. Otherwise the building was dark.

The first thing Ellery saw as they stepped out of the self-service elevator onto the dark third floor was the door of Dean Hope's anteroom . . . wide open.

They found the old scholar crumpled on the floor just inside the doorway. His white hairs dripped red.

"Crook came early," howled Inspector Queen. "Look at the dean's wristwatch, Ellery—smashed in his fall at 7:15."

"I warned him not to unlock his door," wailed Ellery. Then he bellowed. "He's breathing! Call an ambulance!"

He had carried the dean's frail body to a couch in the inner office and was gently wetting the blue lips from a paper cup when the Inspector turned from the telephone.

The eyes fluttered open. "Ellery . . ."

"Doc, what happened?"

"Book . . . taken . . ." The voice trailed off in a mutter.

"Book taken?" repeated the Inspector incredulously. "That means Mimms not only came early, but Dr. Hope found the book was genuine! Is the money on him, son?"

Ellery searched the dean's pockets, the office, the anteroom. "It's gone."

"Then he did buy it. Then somebody came along, cracked him on the skull, and lifted the book."

"Doc!" Ellery bent over the old man again. "Doc, who struck you? Did you see?"

"Yes . . . Gorman . . ." Then the battered head rolled to one side and Dr. Hope lost consciousness.

"Gorman? Who's Gorman, Ellery?"

"Professor Oswald Gorman," Ellery said through his teeth, "one of the English faculty at the lunch today. *Get him.*"

When Inspector Queen returned to the dean's office guiding the agitated elbow of Professor Gorman, he found Ellery waiting behind the dean's flower vase as if it were a bough from Birnam Wood.

The couch was empty.

"What did the ambulance doctor say, Ellery?"

"Concussion. How bad they don't know yet." Ellery rose, fixing Professor Gorman with a Macduffian glance. "And where did you find this pedagogical louse, Dad?"

"Upstairs on the seventh floor, teaching a Bible class."

"The title of my course, Inspector Queen," said the Professor furiously, "is *The Influence of the Bible on English Literature.*"

"Trying to establish an alibi, eh?"

"Well, son," said his father in a troubled voice, "the professor's more than just tried. He's done it."

"Established an alibi?" Ellery cried.

"It's a two-hour seminar, from six to eight. He's alibied for every second from 6 P.M. on by the dozen people taking the course—including a minister, a priest, and a rabbi. What's more," mused the Inspector, "even assuming the 7:15 on the dean's broken watch was a plant, Professor Gorman can account for every minute of his day since your lunch broke up. Ellery, something is rotten in New York County."

"I beg your pardon," said a British voice from the anteroom. "I was to meet Dr. Hope here at eight o'clock."

Ellery whirled. Then he swooped down upon the owner of the voice, a pale skinny man in a bowler hat carrying a package under one arm.

"Don't tell me you're Alfred Mimms and you're just bringing the Bacon!"

"Yes, but I'll—I'll come back," stammered the visitor, trying to hold on to his package. But it was Ellery who won the tug of war, and as he tore the wrappings away the pale man turned to run.

And there was Inspector Queen in the doorway with his pistol showing. "Alfred Mimms, is it?" said the Inspector genially. "Last time, if memory serves, it was Lord Chalmerston. Remember, Dink, when you were sent up for selling a phony First Folio to that Oyster Bay millionaire? Ellery, this is Dink Chalmers of Flatbush, one of the cleverest confidence men in the rare book game." Then the Inspector's geniality faded. "But, son, this leaves us in more of a mess than before."

"No, Dad," said Ellery. "This clears the mess up."

From Inspector Queen's expression, it did nothing of the kind.

"Because what did Doc Hope reply when I asked him what happened?" Ellery said. "He replied, 'Book taken.' Well, obviously, the book wasn't taken. The book was never here. Therefore he didn't mean to say 'book taken.' Professor, you're a communicant of the Matthew Arnold Hope Cult of Spoonerisms: What must the dean have meant to say?"

" 'Took . . . Bacon'!" said Professor Gorman.

"Which makes no sense, either, unless we recall, Dad, that his voice trailed off. As if he meant to add a word, but failed. Which word? The word 'money'—'took Bacon *money*.' Because while the Bacon book wasn't here to be taken, the ten thousand dollars Doc Hope was toting around all day to pay for it was.

"And who took the Bacon money? The one who knocked on the dean's door just after seven o'clock and asked to be let in. The one who, when Dr. Hope unlocked the door—indicating the knocker was someone he knew and trusted—promptly clobbered the old man and made off with his life's savings."

"But when you asked who hit him," protested the Inspector, "he answered 'Gorman'."

"Which he couldn't have meant, either, since the professor has an alibi of granite. Therefore—"

"Another spoonerism!" exclaimed Professor Gorman.

"I'm afraid so. And since the only spoonerism possible from the name 'Gorman' is 'Morgan,' hunt up Mr. Morgan Naseby of the underpaid English Department, Dad, and you'll have Doc's assailant and his ten grand back, too."

Later, at Bellevue Hospital, an indestructible Elizabethan scholar squeezed the younger Queen's hand feebly. Conversation was forbidden, but the good pedagogue and spoonerist extraordinary did manage to whisper, "My queer Dean . . ."

MURDER DEPT.

Driver's Seat

THERE WERE FOUR Brothers brothers until Big Dave died. And then there were three, and that was a bad day for all of them. With Big Dave in the driver's seat there had never been any question of where they were going. The withdrawal of his guiding arm left Archibald, Everett, and Charlton Brothers steering with their noses. They were bound to land in a ditch sooner or later. Big Dave's widow saw to it that it was sooner. . . .

But that is the story.

It was the afternoon of the semiannual board meeting of

the Four Brothers Mining Company. The widow had in-
herited her husband's quarter holdings in the closed corporation, so now—for the fourth consecutive time—she occupied
Big Dave's big chair. And she almost filled it. She was a large
young woman with long legs and very blonde hair in albumi-
nous swirls, and her figure was as rich and ornamented as a
French pastry.

The three brothers did not mind her presence; it gave a
fillip to what had always been a tedious necessity. Or, at least,
Archibald and Everett did not mind; about Charlton it was
difficult to say, for he had the mummified exterior and dyspep-
tic potential of a hot pepper drying on a wall. But Archibald
was like a hairless Santa Claus, leanly ruddy and roaring, the
nearly visible pack on his back crammed with long-legged
blonde memories; and he amused himself by tossing his gusty
gifts at Daisy Brothers across the board table as if she were his
wife's upstairs maid and his wife were at Newport. Everett
toyed with the widow typically, in smiling silence; he was a
mouth-smiler, this Everett Brothers, with cold gray skin and
blunt eyes.

But the widow paid no attention to either Archibald or
Everett; she did not even appear to be listening to the crabby
nose tones of Charlton, who was presiding.

Until Charlton snapped, "If there's no further new business,
I'll entertain a motion—"

Then Daisy Brothers looked away from the oil painting of
Big Dave above Charlton's skimpy hair, and she said: "But
there is."

Archibald stopped frisking, Everett's smile took on an edge
of interest, Charlton raised his sandpapery brows almost audi-

bly. They looked at one another as if the polished table had given tongue; and then they looked at her.

"The Four Brothers Mining Company was organized with one hundred shares of stock divided into four equal blocks," said Big Dave's widow. "That is, each of you and Dave put up $25,000 for twenty-five shares. Today the corporation's holdings are worth a hundred times the original investment."

"Hear, hear," roared Archibald.

"Yes, yes, Daisy," grunted Charlton, beginning to rise.

But Everett, still smiling, put his hand on his desiccated brother's arm.

"Since Dave's death," continued the young widow, "you three lads have gone haywire. My irresistible brother-in-law Archibald here, for instance, he's been taken to the cleaners by a big parade of cuties. Everett, you've gone over your wise-guy head in hock to the bookies and gamblers. And Charlton, you've got a headache to bellyache about for a change; without Dave to tell you what to do, you've lost your shirt in the stock market. And in the meantime your wives have kept throwing money around as if the company mines diamonds instead of coal.

"So for quite a while now each one of you has been in a nice deep hole. And for quite a while now each one of you has been trying to dig himself out by selling part of his stock in the Four Brothers Mining Company."

The brothers made little noises.

Daisy Brothers opened her bag and consulted a slip of paper. "Archibald, the great lover: Arch, you've sold nine of your twenty-five shares. Everett, the big brain: Ev, you've sold seven of your twenty-five. And little Napoleon—Charlton, I mean—you've sold ten of yours."

There was a silence. Then Archibald laughed. "I never knew a head went with those shoulders."

Everett said nothing, but his smile was thoughtful.

"So I wasn't the only one," rasped Charlton, glaring about at his brothers. "Daisy, what's the point?"

"In the original agreement you and Dave all signed," replied the widow briskly, "there's a certain clause that was put in to prevent just what's happened. The clause says that if any partner in the corporation gets stock control, *he can buy out the others at the original cost of their stock.*"

The brothers jerked.

Charlton showed his spiked teeth. "What about it? No one's got stock control of the company!"

"Wrong, brother-in-law," said the sister-in-law. "The shares you three sold were bought through dummies . . . *by me.* Your ten, Charlton. Your seven, Everett. Your nine, Archibald. That's twenty-six shares I bought up from the three of you. And I own Dave's twenty-five. Add it up. It's fifty-one, and it gives me legal control.

"And," said the woman, very gently, "I'm exercising my rights under the agreement." She rummaged in her bag. "I have here," she said, "three certified checks. A $16,000 check for your remaining shares, Archibald. An $18,000 check for your remaining eighteen shares, Everett. And a $15,000 check for your remaining fifteen shares, Charlton. Pony up that stock."

When Archibald found his voice, it came out blasting. "Sixteen thousand! Why, my sixteen shares are worth more than a million and a half! Do you think you can buy me out at one cent on the dollar?"

"I'll let your lawyer answer that question."

Charlton Brothers was purple to the tips of his ears. "Everett," he spluttered, "do you remember anything like that in the original agreement? Is this—is she right?"

Everett nodded, his eyes on the widow.

Charlton snarled. With his pale lips curled, he looked like an aroused vegetable. "Why, you cheap . . . ! You don't think you're going to get away with this!"

"Shut up, Charlton." Archibald came around the table to slip his arm about her shoulders. "Why don't you and I go somewhere, baby, and . . . talk this over?"

She got up so suddenly that the handsome brother almost lost his balance. "I'll give you three exactly one week to let your lawyers convince you that you'd be crazy to try to break that agreement in court. They'll tell you you haven't a prayer, but I guess you'll want to be told." She dropped the three checks into her bag, and turned to go.

But now Everett was on his feet, and he spoke for the first time. "One question, Daisy."

"Yes?"

"Why?"

Daisy Brothers leaned on the table, and its high gloss reflected something bitter, and triumphant, too. "Big Dave took me out of the strip stable in the Boom Boom Club. He was a good businessman, Dave was. He knew a bargain when he saw one. He bought me for a two-buck license and a five-dollar bill to the J. P. and he always said I turned out the best deal he'd ever made. Well, he was right. He gave me respectability, and I gave him the ten happiest years of his life.

"And I'd have been happy, too—if not for you three and your grand dames. From the way you and your wives have treated me, anybody'd think Dave married a dead whale. No class. Didn't know all the forks. Took my degree at Roseland, and postgraduate work stripping in front of a bunch of drunks. It wasn't as if I didn't care. I tried, hard. I tried not to shame you. I even took lessons in how to come into a room without reaching for a zipper. But I was poison. . . . If it was just you jerks, I wouldn't have minded so much. But those highclass babes of yours really gave it to me, and that I couldn't take. For Dave's sake I couldn't take it. I was his wife, and his wife deserved to be treated by his family like a lady, even if she wasn't one. I made up my mind that if I ever got the chance to pay you back . . ."

Big Dave's widow straightened up, breathing as if she had been running. But when she spoke again, her voice flowed as evenly as a high-voltage wire.

"One week from today you three be at my house between two and three in the afternoon. With your stock."

Ellery found his father standing outside the David Brothers mansion on the East River. It had been raining since morning and Ellery had to splash through puddles on the driveway before he could join the Inspector under the porte-cochere.

"Was this trip necessary?" grumbled Ellery, shaking the rain from his hat. "And if so, why couldn't the taxi deposit me decently under the roof?" The protected part of the driveway was roped off.

"Tire tracks," said Inspector Queen. "I thought you'd want to sit in on this, Ellery. It's murder, it's nasty, and . . . I don't know."

Ellery perked up and looked at the tire marks. "Who, how, when, why, and so forth?"

"Mrs. Daisy Brothers, ex-club stripper. Stabbed to death between two and three this P.M. by one of her three brothers-in-law. I've got the whole story from her lawyer." And the Inspector told Ellery of the Four Brothers Mining Company board meeting of the previous week and Big Dave's widow's stock coup. "So I guess they found she was right when she told them they'd be wasting their time and money trying to beat her in court—and as a result she's lying in there in her library, still with the three certified checks, the deadest dame you ever saw. She was alone in the house—she'd given up all her servants when her husband died and she's been living here ever since like a hermit, doing her own work."

"What about these tire marks?"

"Three cars rolled up here one at a time," said Inspector Queen with a sigh. "The marks identify the cars as a Cadillac, a Rolls-Royce, and a Chevrolet—and from the overlapping of the treads, they came in that order. The Caddy is a '51 town car belonging to the finance company—I mean Charlton Brothers; the Rolls is a secondhand job Everett Brothers picked up cheap in London last year; the Chevvy is what Archibald Brothers runs around in when he's calling on his girl friends or otherwise doesn't want to be noticed by some vulgar columnist.

"I've sweated the three gents and they've admitted coming here between two and three today, separately and alone, about fifteen-twenty minutes apart."

"And their stories are?" murmured Ellery.

"Identical. It's collusion, of course; they were all ready for me. They probably drew lots, and the brother who got tagged for the party is being covered up by the other two. Each one says she was already dead when he got here, and that he got scared and ran."

"They'd have to say that," said Ellery reflectively, "otherwise how would they account for their stocks' not having been turned over to her? Let's have a look at the lady."

Big Dave's widow was a mess. Whichever brother had stabbed her with the hunting-knife letter opener from Big Dave's desk, he had wielded it with passion and without finesse, many times.

"But," as the Inspector remarked, "he wasn't out for a medal in technique. The things people do for money!"

"What's this?" Ellery had picked up a man's raincoat with the eraser end of a pencil. The raincoat was slightly damp, the lower part of the right sleeve was rain-soaked, and the front of the coat was smeared untidily and redly. It was of medium size, not new.

"We found it rolled up under that leather chair," said the Inspector. "She fought for her life and he got her blood all over his coat. Rather than risk being caught or even seen with the coat in this condition, he left it here."

"A bad mistake," said Ellery.

"You think so? You won't find any identifying marks, the pockets were cleaned out even of lint and dust, all three brothers owned raincoats like this at one time or other, and they all wear a medium size. Each one denies it's his coat, and each one says he can't produce his own coat because he discarded it long ago. So we don't get at him through elimination."

"There are other ways," remarked Ellery.

"Yes," said his father with a shrug, "we'll do a sweat, hair, and dust analysis, but they're not always conclusive. I have a hunch, son, we won't get any more out of the coat than we did out of the knife, which doesn't show a print."

"I disagree."

"You see something I missed?" exclaimed Inspector Queen. "In the coat?"

"Yes, Dad. Something that indicates exactly which brother killed Big Dave's widow. And with nothing up my sleeve," said Ellery with a grin, "although with something definitely up *his*.

"Look at this coat. It's slightly damp from the rain, but the lower part of the right sleeve is rain-*soaked*. How did that part of the sleeve get soaked while the rest of the sleeve—in fact, the rest of the coat—merely got a little damp?

"The brothers came here separately, at different times, each alone in his car. It's rained all day. So the wearer of this coat drove a car in the rain. In driving a car in the rain, especially in city traffic, what do you habitually do which will get one of your coat sleeves wet?"

"Give arm signals for stops and turns . . . !" But then Inspector Queen looked puzzled. "But the driver always signals with his left arm, Ellery, and it's the right sleeve of this coat that's rain-soaked."

"Conclusion: This driver signalled with his right arm."

"But to be able to do that—" the Inspector stopped. Then he said, slowly, "*His car has a righthand drive.*"

"Charlton's Cadillac and Archibald's Chevrolet—American cars—lefthand drives," said Ellery, nodding. "But the other car is a Rolls-Royce—British; and what's more, a Rolls bought secondhand in London, so it has to have a righthand drive. Indicating the owner of the Rolls—Everett Brothers.

"By the way, Dad, what's he look like?"

PARK PATROL DEPT.

A Lump of Sugar

I F NOT FOR the fact that Mounted Patrolman Wilkins was doing the dawn trick on the bridle path, where it goes by the Park Tavern, the Shakes Cooney murder would never have been solved. Ellery admits this cheerfully. He can afford to, since it was he who brought to that merry-go-round some much-needed horse sense.

A waiter with a hot date had neglected to strip one of his tables on the Tavern's open terrace at closing time the night before, whereupon the question was: Who had done a carving job on Cooney's so-called heart about 6 A.M. the next morning?

Logic said nearly eight million people, or roughly the population of New York City, the law-abiding majority of whom
might well have found Shakes Cooney's continued existence
a bore. But Mounted Patrolman Wilkins was there when it
counted, and it was he who collared the three gentlemen who,
curiously, were in the neighborhood of the deserted Tavern
and Cooney's corpse at that ungentlemanly hour.

Their collars were attached to very important necks, and
when Inspector Richard Queen of police headquarters took
over he handled them, as it were, with lamb's-wool knuckles.
It was not every morning that Inspector Queen was called
upon in a homicide to quiz a statesman, a financial titan, and
an organization politician; and the little Inspector rose to the
occasion.

Senator Kregg responded loftily, as to a reporter from an
opposition newspaper.

Piers d'I. Millard responded remotely, as to a minority stock-
holder.

The Hon. Stevens responded affably, as to a precinct worker.

Lofty, remote, or affable, the three distinguished suspects in
riding clothes agreed in their stories to the tittle of an iota.
They had been out for an early canter on the bridle path.
They had not addressed or seen any fourth person until the
mounted policeman gathered them in. The life and death of
Shakes Cooney were as nothing to them. Patrolman Wilkins's
act in detaining them had been "totalitarian"—Senator Kregg;
"ill-advised"—Financier Millard; "a sucker play"—Politician
Stevens.

Delicately, Inspector Queen broached certain possibly rele-
vant matters, *viz.*: In the national forest of politics, it was
rumored, Senator Kregg (ex-Senator Kregg) was being meas-

ured as a great and spreading oak, of such timber as presidents
are made. Financier Piers d'I. Millard was said to be the Senator's architect, already working on the blueprints with his
golden stylus. And small-souled political keyholers would have
it that the Hon. Stevens was down on the plans as sales manager of the development. Under the circumstances, said the
Inspector with a cough, some irreverent persons might opine
that Shakes Cooney—bookie, tout, gambler, underworld slug,
and clubhouse creep, with the instincts of a jay and the ethics
of a grave robber—had learned of the burial place of some
body or other, the exhumation of which would so befoul the
Senator's vicinity as to wither his noble aspirations on the
branch. It might even be surmised, suggested Inspector Queen
apologetically, that Cooney's price for letting the body stay
buried was so outrageous as to cause Someone to lose his head.
Would the gentlemen care to comment?

The Senator obliged in extended remarks, fortunately off
the record, then he surged away. Prepared to totter after,
Financier Millard paused long enough to ask reflectively, "And
how long, did you say, Inspector Queen, you have been with
the New York police department?"—and it sounded like the
coup de grâce to an empire. The Hon. Stevens lingered to ooze
a few lubricating drops and then he, too, was gone.

When Ellery arrived on the scene he found his father in a
good, if thoughtful, temper. The hide, remarked Inspector
Queen, was pretty much cut-and-dried; the question was, To
whose door had Shakes been trying to nail it? Because Shakes
Cooney hadn't been a man to take murder lying down. The
evidence on the Tavern terrace showed that after his assailant
fled Cooney had struggled to his hands and knees, the Tavern
steak knife stuck in his butchered chest, and that he had gorily

crawled—kept alive by sheer meanness, protested the Inspector
—to the table which the preoccupied waiter had forgotten to
clear off the night before; that the dying man had then reached
to the table top and groped for a certain bowl; and that from
this bowl he had plucked the object which they had found in
his fist, a single lump of sugar. Then, presumably with satisfaction, Shakes had expired.

"He must have been one of your readers," complained the
Inspector. "Because, Ellery, that's a dying message or I'm the
Senator's uncle. But which one was Shakes fingering?"

"Sugar," said Ellery absently. "In Cooney's dictionary sugar
means—"

"Sure. But Millard isn't the only one of the three who's
loaded with heavy sugar. The ex-Senator's well stocked, and
he recently doubled his inventory by marrying that fertilizer
millionaire's daughter. And Stevens has the first grand he ever
grafted. So Shakes didn't mean that kind of sugar. What's
sugar mean in *your* dictionary, son?"

Ellery, who had left page 87 of his latest novel in his typewriter, picked the lint off his thoughts. Finally he said, "Get
me the equestrian history of Kregg, Millard, and Stevens," and
he went back home to literature.

That afternoon his father phoned from Center Street.

"What?" said Ellery, frowning over at his typewriter.

"About their horseback riding," snapped the Inspector.
"The Senator used to ride, but he had a bad fall ten years ago
and now he only punishes a saddle in the gym—the electrical
kind. Moneybags hasn't been on the back of a plug since he
walked out on Grandpa Millard's plowhorse in '88, in Indi-
ana. Only reason Piers d'I. allowed himself to be jockeyed into
those plush-lined jodhpurs this morning, I'm pretty sure, is so

he, Kregg, and Stevens could have a nice dirty skull session in the Park out of range of the newsreel cameras."

"And Stevens?"

"That bar insect?" snorted the old gentleman. "Only horse *he* knows how to ride is a dark one, with galluses. This morning's the first time Stevens ever set his suède-topped brogans into a stirrup."

"Well, well," said Ellery, sounding surprised. "Then what did Shakes mean? Sugar . . . Is one of them tied up with the sugar industry in some way? Has Kregg ever been conspicuous in sugar legislation? Is Millard a director of some sugar combine? Or maybe Stevens owns some sugar stock. Try that line, Dad."

His father said wearily, "I don't need you for that kind of fishing, my son. That's in the works."

"Then you're in," said Ellery; and without enjoyment he went back to his novel which, like Shakes Cooney, was advancing on its hands and knees.

Two days later Inspector Queen telephoned his report. "Not one of them is tied up with sugar in any way whatsoever. Only connection Kregg, Millard, and Stevens have with the stuff is what I take it they drop into their coffee." After a moment the Inspector said, "Are you there?"

"Lump of sugar," Ellery mumbled. "And Shakes evidently thought it would be clear . . ." The mumble ended in a glug.

"Yes?" said his father, brightening.

"Of course," chuckled Ellery. "Dad, get a medical report on those three. Then let me know which one of 'em has diabetes."

The Inspector's uppers clacked against his lowers. "That's my baby! That's it, son! It's as good as wrapped up!"

The following day Inspector Queen phoned again.

"Whose father?" asked Ellery, running his fingers through his hair. "Oh! Yes, Dad? What is it?"

"About the case, Ellery—"

"Case? Oh, the case. Yes? Well? Which one's diabetic?"

The Inspector said thoughtfully, "None."

"None! You mean—?"

"I mean."

"Hmm," said Ellery. "Hnh!"

For some time Inspector Queen heard nothing but little rumbles, pops, flutters, and other ruminative noises, until suddenly the line was cleared by a sound as definite as the electrocutioner's switch.

"You've got something?" said the Inspector doubtfully.

"Yes. Yes," said Ellery, with no doubt whatever, but considerable relief. "Yes, Dad, now I know whom Shakes Cooney meant!"

"Who?" demanded the Inspector.

"We ruled out all the reasonable interpretations of sugar," said Ellery, "leaving us where we started—with a lump of sugar in Cooney's clutch as a clue to his killer. Since the fancy stuff is out, suppose we take a lump of sugar in a man's hand to mean just that: a lump of sugar in a man's hand. Why does a man carry a lump of sugar with him?"

"I give up," said the Inspector promptly. "Why?"

"Why?" said Ellery. "Why, to feed it to a horse."

"Feed it to a—" The old gentleman was silent. Then he said, "So that's why you wanted to know their riding history. But Ellery, that theory fizzled. None of the three is what you'd call a horseman, so none of the three would be likely to have a lump of sugar on him."

"Absolutely correct," said Ellery. "So Shakes was indicating a fourth suspect, only I didn't see it then. Cooney was a bookie and a gambler. You'll probably find that this fellow was over his noggin in Cooney's book, couldn't pay off, and took the impulsive way out—"

"Wait, hold it!" howled his father. "*Fourth* suspect? What fourth suspect?"

"Why, the fourth man on the bridle path that morning. And he *would* be likely to carry a lump of sugar for his horse."

"*Mounted Patrolman Wilkins!*"

OPEN FILE DEPT.

Cold Money

THE HOTEL CHANCELLOR in midtown New York is not likely to forget the two visits of Mr. Philly Mullane. The first time Mullane registered at the Chancellor, under the name of Winston F. Parker, an alert house detective spotted him and, under the personal direction of Inspector Richard Queen, Philly was carried out of Room 913, struggling and in bracelets, to be tried, convicted, and sentenced to ten years for a Manhattan payroll robbery. The second time—ten years later —he was carried out neither struggling nor manacled, inasmuch as he was dead.

The case really began on a blacktop county road east of Route 7 in the Berkshire foothills, when Mullane sapped his pal Mikie the Waiter over the left ear and tossed him out of their getaway car, thereby increasing the split from thirds to halves. Mullane was an even better mathematician than that. Five miles farther north, he administered the same treatment to Pittsburgh Patience, which left him sole proprietor of their $62,000 haul. Mikie and Patience were picked up by Connecticut state police; the Waiter was speechless with rage, which could not be said of Patience, a lady of inspired vocabulary. Three weeks later Philly Mullane was smoked out of the Chancellor room where he had been skulking. The payroll was absent—in those three weeks the $62,000 had vanished. He had not blown the money in, for the checkback showed that he had made for the New York hotel immediately on ditching his confederates.

Question: Where had Mullane stashed the loot?

Everyone wanted to know. In the case of Pittsburgh Patience and Mikie the Waiter, their thirst for information had to go unsatisfied; they drew ten-year sentences, too. As for the police, for all their success in locating the stolen banknotes, they might as well have gone up the river with Mullane and his steaming ex-associates.

They tried everything on Mullane, including a planted cellmate. But Mullane wasn't talking, even in his sleep.

The closest they came was in the sixth year of Philly's stretch. In July of that year, in the exercise yard, Philly let out a yell that he had been stabbed, and he collapsed. The weapon which had stabbed him was the greatest killer of all, and when he regained consciousness in the infirmary the prison doctor named it for him. It was his heart.

"My pumper?" Mullane said incredulously. "Me?" And then he looked scared, and he said in a weak voice, "I want to see the Warden."

The Warden came at once; he was a kindly man who wished his rough flock well, but he had been waiting for this moment for over five years. "Yes, Mullane?" the Warden said.

"About that sixty-two grand," whispered Philly.

"Yes, Mullane?" the Warden said.

"I never been a boy scout, God knows—"

"Yes, He does," said the Warden.

"That's what I mean, Warden. I mean, I figure I can't take it with me, and maybe I can cut down on that book He's keeping on me upstairs. I guess I better tell you where I stashed that dough. The doc tells me I'm going to die—"

But the prison doctor was young and full of Truth and other ideals, and he interrupted indignantly, "I said *eventually*. Not now, Mullane! You may not get another attack for years."

"Oh?" said Philly in a remarkably strong voice. "Then what am I worried about?" And he grinned at the Warden and turned his face to the wall.

The Warden could have kicked both of them.

So everybody settled back to more waiting.

What they were waiting for was Mullane's release. They had plenty of time—the law, Patience, the Waiter, and Mullane most of all. Having behaved themselves as guests of the state, Patience and Mikie got out in something over seven years, and they went their respective ways. Mullane's silence stuck him for the limit.

The day he was released the Warden said to him, "Mullane, you'll never get away with that money. And even if you should, nobody ever gets anything out of money that doesn't belong to him."

"I figure I've earned it, Warden," said Philly Mullane with a crooked smile. "At that, it only comes to a measly sixty-two hundred a year."

"What about your heart?"

"Ah, that doc was from hunger."

Of course, they put a twenty-four hour tail on him. And they lost him. Two headquarters detectives were demoted because of it. When he was found ten days later he had been dead about fifteen minutes.

A long memory and a smart bit of skull work on the part of one of the Hotel Chancellor's house dicks, Blauvelt, were responsible for the quick discovery of the body. Blauvelt had been on a two-week vacation. When he returned to duty, the hotel staff was yakking about a guest named Worth who had checked in nine days before and had not left his room since. The only ones who had seen him were the room service people—he had all his meals served in his room—the chambermaid, and a few bellboys. They reported that he kept his door not only locked day and night, but on the chain. The room was 913, and a desk clerk recalled that Worth had insisted on that room and no other.

"I only came on the job this morning, so I haven't been able to get a look at him," Blauvelt said over the phone to police headquarters, "but from what they tell me, except for a change in the color of his hair and a couple inches in height, which could be elevators, he answers the description. Inspector, if this Worth ain't Philly Mullane hiding out I'll get me a job in the Sanitation Department."

"Nice going, Blauvelt. We'll be right over." Inspector Queen hung up and said admiringly, "Same hotel, same room. You've got to hand it to him—" But then he stopped.

"Exactly," said Ellery, who had been listening on the extension. He remembered the case as one of his father's pet bogies. "It's too smart. Unless that's where he hid the money in the first place."

"But Ellery, that room at the Chancellor was searched when we grabbed Mullane off ten years ago!"

"Not the super de luxe type search I recommend in such cases," mourned Ellery. "Remember how cleverly Mullane led you to believe he'd buried the money during his getaway? He had you digging up half the cornfields in Connecticut! Dad, it's been in that room at the Chancellor all this time."

So they went up to the Chancellor with Sergeant Velie and a couple of precinct men and Blauvelt unlocked the door of 913 with his passkey. The door was off the chain, the reason for which became immediately clear when they saw that Mullane had been murdered.

The precinct men went scurrying, and Sergeant Velie got busy on the phone.

Mullane was in a chair at the writing desk in a corner of the bedroom, his face and arms on the desk. He had been cracked on the back of the head with some heavy object which a quick examination told them was not there. From the contusion, the Inspector guessed it had been a hammer.

"But this wound doesn't look as if the blow was hard enough to have caused death," frowned Ellery.

"Mullane's ticker went bad in prison," said his father. "Bad heart, hard blow—curtains."

Ellery looked around. The room had not yet been made up for the day and it was in some disorder. He began to amble, mumbling to himself. "Wouldn't have hidden it in a piece of furniture—they're moved around in hotels all the time. . . . In *nothing* removable . . . Walls and ceiling tinted plaster— would mean replastering, duplicating the tint . . . too risky . . ." He got down on all fours and began crawling about.

The Inspector was at the desk. "Blauvelt. Help me sit him up."

The body was still warm and the house detective had to hold on to keep it from collapsing. Mullane's dressing gown sleeves and collar were a mess of wet blue ink. He had been writing a note of some kind and in falling forward had upset the ink bottle.

The Inspector stiffened. He looked around for a towel, but there was none in the bedroom.

"Velie, get some used towels from the bathroom. Maybe we can sop up enough of this wet ink to make out what Mullane was writing!"

"No used towels in here," called the Sergeant from the bathroom.

"Then get clean ones, you dimwit!"

Velie came out with some unused towels, and Inspector Queen went to work on the note. He worked for five minutes, delicately. But all he could show for it were three shaky words: *Money hidden in* . . . The rest was blotted beyond recall.

"Why would he write where the dough was stashed?" wondered Blauvelt, continuing to embrace Mullane.

"Because after he got up this morning," snapped the Inspector, "he must have felt a heart attack coming on. When he got his attack in prison, he almost spilled to the Warden. This time it probably scared him so much he sat right down and wrote the hiding place of the money. Then he slumped forward, unconscious or dying. Killer got in—maybe thought he was dozing—finished him off, read the note before the ink soaked all the way in—"

"And found the loot," said Ellery, from under the bed. "It's gone, Dad."

So Blauvelt let Mullane go and they all got down on their faces and saw the neat hole in the floor, under the rug, with an artistically fitted removable board, where the payroll had lain for ten years. The hole was empty.

When they got to their feet, Ellery was no longer with them. He was stooping over what was left of Mullane.

"Ellery, what are you *doing?*" exclaimed Inspector Queen.

Even Sergeant Velie looked repelled. Ellery was running his palm over the dead man's cheeks with tenderness.

"Nice," he said.

"*Nice!*"

"Nice smooth shave he took this morning. You can still see traces of talc."

Blauvelt's mouth was open.

"You want to learn something, Blauvelt?" said Sergeant Velie with a nudge that doubled the house detective up. "Now it gives a great big deduction."

"Certainly does," grinned Ellery. "It gives the killer of Philly Mullane."

The Sergeant opened his mouth.

"Shut up, Velie," said Inspector Queen. "Well?"

"Because if Mullane shaved this morning," asked Ellery, "where did he do it, Sergeant?"

"Okay, I bite," said Velie. "Where?"

"Where every man shaves, Sergeant, in the bathroom. Ever shave in the bathroom without using a towel?"

"That's easy. What do you think I wipe my face with, the bath mat?"

"All right, Ellery, so Mullane used a towel," said the Inspector impatiently. "So what?"

"So where is it? When you asked Velie to get one from the bathroom to sop up the ink with, Dad, he said *there were no used towels in there*. And there are no towels at all in the bedroom here. What did Velie bring you from the bathroom? Some *unused* towels. In other words, after Mullane shaved this morning, *someone took the dirty towels away and replaced them with clean ones*. And this is a hotel, and Mullane, who always kept the door on the chain, had obviously let someone in . . ."

"*The chambermaid!*"

"Has to be. Mullane let the chambermaid in this morning, as usual, she got to work in the bathroom—and she never did get to the bedroom, as you can see. Why? It can only be because while she was cleaning up in the bathroom Mullane got his heart attack!

"It was the chambermaid who struck Mullane on the back of the head with the hammer she'd brought in with her—waiting for a chance to use it, as she's probably waited every morning for the last nine days.

"It was the chambermaid who read Mullane's message and scooped the payroll money out of the hole in the floor."

"But to have come in with a hammer—she must have planned this, she must have known who he was!"

"Right, Dad. So I think you'll find, when you catch up with her, that the homicidal chambermaid is your old friend, Pittsburgh Patience, with a few alterations in her appearance.

Patience suspected all along where Mullane had hidden the money, and as soon as she was out of stir three years ago she got herself a job on the Chancellor housekeeping staff . . . and waited for her old pal to show up!"

EMBEZZLEMENT DEPT.

The Myna Birds

FRIENDS OF THE feathered world will have no trouble recalling the case of old Mrs. Andrus, who left a million dollars to thirty-eight myna birds. What is not generally known, even among birdlovers, is that Ellery was in that case up to his pectorals, taking wing on as pretty a flight of reasoning as his casebook attests.

With the assistance, be it noted, of the only bird-detective on record.

Mrs. Andrus was a lonely old lady who had outlived family and friends, and whom an aging body had condemned to a wheelchair. Her only human connections were her doctor, her lawyer, and her paid companion. But Dr. Cooke was a bloated man with a sort of decayed charm, like an overripe banana; Attorney De Rose, whom the doctor had recommended to manage Mrs. Andrus's affairs when she became too infirm to manage them herself, was a sporty fellow with a perpetual tan and a voice that hurt the old lady's ears; and her companion, Miss Baggott, also introduced by Dr. Cooke, was a frozen-faced female of doubtful gentility whom Mrs. Andrus tolerated only because the woman tended the birds devotedly. And so the mynas, which had begun as a hobby, became the reason for what was left of the old lady's life.

They were true talking mynas from southern India—pert, hoppy little creatures amusingly yellow-wattled, with iridescent black wings and bass voices. Some of them had vocabularies of almost a hundred words. Mrs. Andrus found them a great comfort—far more satisfactory companions, she thought, than Miss Baggott. Her dependents, she called them; and, quite as if they were, the old lady worried over their fate when she should be gone.

From this it was a logical step to securing their future. Mrs. Andrus directed Attorney De Rose immediately to place the bulk of her property into a fund earmarked for her birds' support, maintenance, and loving care. Mr. De Rose and Dr. Cooke consented to administer the fund, and Miss Baggott was specified as permanent curator. When the last myna should have passed away, the fund was to be administered for the benefit of designated charities.

In the interim, Mrs. Andrus asked little for herself. The attorney paid her bills, she and the mynas were company for each other, and she was content.

Her pets' one failing, Mrs. Andrus sometimes felt, was their inability to play contract bridge, the only other interest of her declining years. For this diversion she had to depend on Dr. Cooke and Mr. De Rose, with Miss Baggott making the fourth. On such evenings as the gentlemen could spare for her entertainment, the old lady would be ensconced in her wheelchair at the bridge table, playing a remarkably shrewd game for a tenth of a cent a point. Her bridge nights completed her happiness.

But on the last night of her life, Mrs. Andrus was not happy. Her usually pleasant face, as she wheeled herself into her living room, was positively menacing. Miss Baggott, who had set up the bridge table and chairs, glanced quickly at the physician and the lawyer.

"Nothing wrong, I hope, Mrs. Andrus?" asked Dr. Cooke genially, waving his cigar. "We're not feeling that nasty pain again tonight, are we?"

"It's nothing a grand slam won't cure—eh, Mrs. Andrus?" roared De Rose. "Well, well, the usual partners?"

"The game," said Mrs. Andrus, not stirring from her doorway, "is over." Behind her, in the bedroom, thirty-eight pairs of unwinking eyes looked on attentively.

"Over?" Miss Baggott half rose.

Hello, funnyface! said a bass voice suddenly from somewhere behind Mrs. Andrus.

"Hush, Minnie," said the old lady, without turning. "You thought I was asleep at my naptime today, Miss Baggott, but you were quite mistaken. I overheard what you said on the phone to Mr. De Rose and Dr. Cooke. Don't you trust your confederates, Miss Baggott? Or have they been cheating their own kind, too?"

"Confederates? Cheating?" said Attorney De Rose heartily.

"I'm sure I don't know what you think you overheard, Mrs. Andrus—" began Dr. Cooke with a smile.

"I overheard enough, Doctor, to realize why you brought Mr. De Rose and Miss Baggott into my life. I'm being systematically robbed by the three of you. I've been an old fool, but not any more! First," said the old lady in the same hard voice, "you're to put back what you've taken. You have ten minutes to give me an accounting of the stolen funds."

"Ten minutes?" said the doctor incredulously.

"Ten minutes, Dr. Cooke. Then we'll go on from there."

Say ah! said another bass voice.

Mrs. Andrus backed her wheelchair swiftly into her bedroom and slammed the door.

The three at the card table were silent for some time. Then Dr. Cooke said pleasantly, "Well, Baggie, you messed it up. Suppose you fix it."

"That's right, blame me," shrilled Miss Baggott. "I warned you two not to be so greedy—to wait till she kicked off! Put the money back. Maybe she won't prosecute—"

"Academic," murmured the doctor. "The bookies have my share. And from the way you've been painting the town, De Rose, I gather you're in the same stable. Any suggestions from our legal department?"

The lawyer extinguished his cigaret in the ashtray before him with a brutal thumb; under his tan, he was livid. "The way I'd fixed it, we could have gone on working this gold mine for years. Who'd squawk—the birds?"

"There's an old bird in that bedroom who's going to squawk. To the D.A.!" said Miss Baggott venomously.

"And suppose she doesn't."

"What?"

"Suppose she doesn't," said the lawyer, squeezing the deck of cards. "Suppose tonight we had to cut our bridge game short because, say, Miss Baggott wasn't feeling well. And suppose Dr. Cooke gave her some sleeping pills, and Miss Baggott retired to her room and went out like a light, and the doctor and Mr. De Rose left. And suppose, as soon as they were gone, that slippery apartment burglar who's been working the West Side lately broke in here. And suppose," said the lawyer, looking up at them, "suppose the old woman surprised him and he lost his stupid head. And suppose, since he's known to carry a knife—"

"No," whispered Miss Baggott. "No."

"Yes," mocked the lawyer. "Unless you want to go to jail for ten years. I don't. Do you, Doctor?"

"Your diagnosis," said Dr. Cooke slowly, "convinces me." Then he said quickly, "Let's agree on the *modus operandi* before she comes back . . ."

Ellery and Inspector Queen broke into the Andrus apartment thirty-five seconds too late. Ellery stopped in the living room to bend over the still bleeding body in the wheelchair while his father, pistol drawn, kicked open the bedroom door to be buffeted by a storm of black wings and bass bird cries. But the Inspector beat his way through in time to catch Dr. Cooke, Attorney De Rose, and Miss Baggott all trying to pile through the same window to get to the fire escape.

The interruption had come so suddenly on the heels of the murder that, while the knife had been wiped clean, there had been no time even to replace it in the kitchen drawer.

Later, when the assistant medical examiner wheeled the

frail corpse into the bedroom for his examination, the myna birds swooped and hopped and chattered about the closed door as if they knew what had happened.

Cut! boomed one bird, a particularly large fellow. *Cut, cut!*

"Yes, Blackie, yes." Ellery picked him up and, stroking his throat feathers, faced the pale manacled trio with cold anger. "Whatever phony plant you animals had in mind, it was doomed to failure before it was even hatched. Mrs. Andrus phoned me early this evening after sending Miss Baggott out on an errand. She told me all about what she'd found out today, and about calling you three together for a showdown tonight. I warned her not to show her hand till we got here, but apparently she was too outraged to wait. And you killed her."

Cut! said the myna bird again.

"Correction noted, birdie," rasped Inspector Queen. "Which one of you did the actual cutting?"

"You've got us all wrong, gentlemen." De Rose's lips were stiff. "The doctor and I arrived late, and Miss Baggott was just coming back from a walk. We all saw a masked man duck out the window. Then you pounded on the door, and we panicked—"

"You don't say, Counselor!"

"There must be some way of telling," mumbled Ellery, walking over to the bridge table. "They came here tonight ostensibly for a bridge game—"

"Hold it, son." The assistant medical examiner was coming out of the bedroom. "Well, Prouty?"

"Four knife wounds, left chest." Dr. Prouty examined the silent trio with the enthusiasm of a funeral director. "No one wound sufficient to cause instant death, but at her age and condition they were cumulatively fatal. . . . What did he say?"

Cut, cut, cut! the big myna was squawking. He struggled, and Ellery let him go. The bird hopped onto the bridge table and began vindictively to peck at a card. After a moment he lost interest and flew off.

"He said 'cut,'" said Dr. Prouty wonderingly. "Why, he must have been an eyewitness to the murder!" He went out, shaking his head.

"Thirty-eight eyewitnesses," said Ellery, gnawing a nail. "Maybe, Dad, we ought to question them."

"I'd almost settle for that," snapped the Inspector. "Only, as it happens, even they weren't here."

"They weren't?" frowned Ellery.

"Not in the living room here, where she got it. I guess you didn't notice. They flew in from the bedroom when I kicked the door open and grabbed these lice. . . . What's the matter with *you?*"

"But if Blackie wasn't on the scene of the crime, why does he keep saying 'Cut'?"

"How should I know?" said the Inspector, exasperated. "It's one of the words he's picked up. Look, son—"

"No, Dad, wait." Then Ellery said softly, "You're right. It's one of the words he picked up because Mrs. Andrus was so fond of bridge . . . she told me herself she played cards with these people regularly—*The cards!*"

And a few minutes later Ellery rose from one of the three chairs at the bridge table, and his voice made Dr. Cooke, Attorney De Rose, and Miss Baggott even paler. "At one point tonight you three sat in these chairs—Mrs. Andrus would have had to use her wheelchair. What were you doing? These cards tell the story. The closed deck in the middle of the table contains forty-nine cards. The three other cards are distributed about the table—one at each of your seats, face up. The three of hearts. The king of spades. The nine of hearts."

"*They cut the cards,*" said the Inspector. "Butchers. Cutting to see which one was going to stick the old lady!"

"This card setup, which you had no time to put away," growled Ellery, "even tells us who drew what. From the cigars in your breast pocket and that cold cigar butt in the ashtray beside the spade king, Dr. Cooke, it was you who drew the king of spades. The cigaret butt in the tray beside the nine of hearts indicates your seat, De Rose, because if it had been smoked by this woman it would be tipped with her lipstick. So you, Miss Baggott, drew the heart three."

"Three, nine, king," rapped the Inspector. "That does it!"

Ellery nodded. "It does indeed."

"It was the skunk who drew the king of spades, of course," said the Inspector. "*You, Cooke.*"

"No," said the doctor urgently.

"No," agreed Ellery. His father wheeled. "No one with medical training, Dad, would stab four times in the area of the heart and fail to hit a vital spot. Dr. Cooke would have finished her in one surgical stroke."

"But Cooke drew the high card," protested the Inspector.

"Then they were cutting for loser, not winner," said Ellery. "So it wasn't the high card that drew the murder assignment, *it was low card.* And since we know De Rose drew the heart nine and you the heart three," he said to the rigid woman, "that lays this miserable killing right in your lap, Miss Baggott."

The big myna made a sudden landing on Miss Baggott's head. She cowered, shrieking.

Down one! rumbled the bird.

"Now that, Blackie, is your first mistake," said Ellery. "Under the laws of this state, it's going to be . . . down three!"

SUICIDE DEPT.

A Question of Honor

It wasn't every day that Ellery found himself meeting a policeman who was a minor authority on Shakespeare, and he shook the hand of Inspector Queen's British visitor with interest. It was a hard hand attached to a squared-off torso, satisfying the professional requirements; but above the neck Inspector Burke of New Scotland Yard took an unexpected turn—broad forehead, pale skin, and the bright, sad eyes of a scholar.

"Over here on a case, Inspector Burke?"

"Yes, and then again no," said the Scotland Yard man

dourly. " 'All hoods make not monks,' as Katherine points out in *Henry VIII.* I'm here hunting a bad one, right enough; but the thing is, he's waiting for me—and, what's more, when I catch the blighter I'm going to have to let him go."

"Why?" asked Ellery, astonished.

"Seems like a long trip, Burke," grinned Inspector Queen, "for mere exercise."

" 'Necessity's sharp pinch,' gentlemen." The Englishman's sad eyes turned sharp. "It's rather a yarn. A certain young woman in London—daughter of someone very highly placed— is shortly to announce her betrothal to a man very much in the international eye. The principals are so distinguished that —well, the match couldn't have been made without the consent of Whitehall, which is all I'm free to say about it at this time.

"A year or so ago this girl, who is charming but headstrong and overromantic," continued the British policeman, "wrote seven highly indiscreet letters to a man with whom she was then infatuated.

"Now the position of the girl's fiancé is such that, should those letters get to him or become public knowledge, he would be forced to break the engagement, and the resulting scandal would almost certainly create a nasty diplomatic situation in an extremely sensitive political area. 'Great floods from simple sources,' you know!

"When the girl's . . . family learned about the letters, they took immediate steps to retrieve them. But there was the rub. The man to whom they'd been written no longer had them. They had just been stolen from him."

"Hm," said Ellery's father.

"No, no, Queen, he's above suspicion. Besides, we know

the identity of the thief. Or rather," said Inspector Burke gloomily, "we're positive he's one of three men."

"Parties of our acquaintance?" asked Ellery.

"Undoubtedly, Mr. Queen, if you've browsed through your Rogues' Gallery recently. They're all Americans. One is the international jewel thief and society impersonator, William Ackley, Jr., alias Lord Rogers, alias le Comte de Crécy; another is the confidence man, J. Phillip Benson, alias John Hammerschmidt, alias Phil the Penman; the third is Walter Chase, the transatlantic cardsharp."

The Queens exchanged glances; Ackley, Benson, and Chase were three of Center Street's incurable headaches.

"When the matter was turned over to the Yard, very hush-hush, I was placed in charge, and I bungled it." Inspector Burke's sensitive face flushed. "Word leaked out that something big was in the wind, and all sorts of mugs with guilty consciences ran for cover before we could tighten our lines. Among them were Benson, Chase, and Ackley—all three got away to the States. One of them—exactly which one we haven't been able to determine—subsequently made contact, with demands and instructions, and I'm here to pay him off."

Inspector Queen clucked. "When and where, Burke?"

"Tonight, in my hotel room. I'm to hand him twenty thousand pounds in American dollars—in exchange, of course, for the letters. So tonight I'll know which of the three he is—and much good will it do me." The Englishman rose, tightening his lips. "And that's my tale of woe, Queen. I must ask you not to go near any of the trio—really my chief reason for stopping by. We can't risk another slip. Those letters must be repossessed and returned to England to be destroyed."

"Can we give you any help?"

"No, no. Unless I botch it again—in which case," said Inspector Burke with a twisted smile, "you might offer me a job sweeping out your office. I shan't feel very happy about going back. . . . Well! Gentlemen, wish me luck."

"Luck," said the Queens in sober unison.

They recalled the bitter twist in Burke's smile the next time they saw him, which was in his hotel room the following morning. A chambermaid had found him. He had been seated slackly in the armchair beside the neatly made bed, a bullet hole in his powder-burned right temple. He had been dead since the night before. No shot had been heard; it was an ultramodern hotel, with soundproof walls. The gun lying on the carpet below his right hand had already been checked in the police laboratory against the slug dug out of his head by the medical examiner.

The room was the picture of peace. A gladstone bag was spread on the luggage rack, undisturbed. The night table held Burke's pipe and tobacco pouch and a dogeared copy of Shakespeare's plays with Burke's signature on the flyleaf. A dispatch case initialed *L. B.* lay, open and empty, on the bed.

"Poor Burke," muttered Inspector Queen. He handed Ellery a sheet of hotel stationery. "Found on the writing table. It has a couple of his fingerprints on it, and it's his handwriting—we've checked."

The script was even and unhurried, as if the brain directing the hand that had written it had reached a decision:

> *"Mine honor is my life; both grow in one;*
> *Take honor from me, and my life is done."*
>
> —LESTER BURKE

"Epitaph by Shakespeare," murmured Ellery. "What went wrong, Dad?"

"Apparently his man came last night with the letters, as agreed, but while Burke checked them over—probably turning away slightly—the rat sapped him; Doc says there's a slight contusion toward the back of Burke's head. Then the double-crosser took the money *and* the letters, and skipped. Guess he figures those highborn pash notes are good for at least one more transatlantic squeeze when the heat dies down, and meanwhile he's got some fifty-odd grand to tide him over. And when poor old Burke came to and realized what he'd let happen— and all it meant—he couldn't face the disgrace and committed suicide."

"There's no doubt it is suicide?"

"You name it. Bullet fired in contact with Burke's temple, angle of entry checks for a righthanded man, slug from Burke's own gun found in the body, Burke's prints on the stock. Suicide note in Burke's authenticated handwriting. Letters not here. Money taken. It's suicide, all right—the only question is which one of those three cuties crossed Burke up and drove him to it . . . Ackley, Chase, or Benson."

Benson, a gray-haired, dapper little man with a Florida tan, was located in a barbershop on Park Row having his nails manicured. The confidence man looked like a Wall Street broker or a corporation executive. He seemed annoyed.

"Don't know what you're talking about, Inspector," Benson snapped. "I can account for every second of my time all day yesterday until well after midnight. I was up in Westchester looking over some property with two associates of mine, we had dinner and spent the evening discussing the deal at the home of one of them in White Plains, and the other one drove me back to my apartment in town—dropped me off a few minutes past one A.M. Their names? Certainly!"

Benson's associates turned out to be two confidence men with slightly lesser reputations. However, they corroborated Benson's story, which was all Inspector Queen was interested in at the moment.

Chase was located in a midtown hotel at the tail end of an all-night poker game—a big, soft-spoken rancher type of man, whose drawl and slow movements ingeniously drew attention from the smooth lightning of his long white hands. No pigeon was being plucked; Chase's companions were professional gamblers.

"Relaxation," smiled the cardsharp. "Man gets tired playin' with rank amateurs. Last night, Inspector? Why, I've been right here since we started our game four o'clock yesterday afternoon. Haven't left this room. Have I, boys?"

Four heads shook emphatically.

That seemed to make it Ackley, whom they found at breakfast in a triplex Park Avenue apartment with its owner, a bejeweled society widow who was outraged at the interruption. Ackley was a tall, lean, handsome man with dark curly hair and piercing black eyes.

"Ackley?" echoed the lady furiously. "This gentleman is Lord Rogers, the big-game hunter, and his lordship has been entertaining me since the cocktail hour yesterday afternoon with his fascinating adventures in Kenya and Tanganyika—"

"Continuously, madam?" asked Inspector Queen politely.

"I ah—put him up for the night," said the lady, coloring. "We—he retired at two A.M. Will you please get out!"

"After you, your lordship," said the Inspector; and the jewel thief shrugged and went along.

Ellery followed in troubled silence.

He was not to break that silence for a long time. For the three alibis remained unshaken, and Ackley, Chase, and Benson had to be released for lack of evidence.

"One of those alibis is rigged!" yelped the Inspector. "But which one?"

The letters and the money failed to turn up.

Inspector Queen raged and fumed, but the case had to be written off. Ellery fumed, too, but for other reasons. Something about the circumstances of Burke's death was wrong, he felt in his bones, but what it was he simply could not diagnose. And Inspector Burke's body and effects were shipped back to England, and the cables from London suddenly stopped, and that seemed the end of it.

But it was not, and it broke out again in the oddest way. One night, weeks later, Inspector Queen came home bemoaning the deterioration of the new generation of police officers. They had all reverted to childhood, the Inspector snorted at dinner, spending their spare time at headquarters playing games.

"Games?" said Ellery.

"Crime puzzles. They make 'em up and challenge one another to solve 'em. They've even got the Chief Inspector doing it! Though come to think of it," the Inspector chuckled, "one he tossed at me today is pretty darn clever. Typical detective-story situation: Rich man with three no-good heirs who need money bad. He's bumped off, one of the three did it, and each claims an alibi for the time of the murder. One says he was in the Museum of Art looking at some eighteenth-century American paintings. The second says he was dialing his bookie's private phone number, Aqueduct 4–2320, putting down a horse bet. The third says he was in a Flatbush bar talking to a French sailor named Socrates Papadapolis who was on his way to Indo-China. Question: Which alibi was the sure-enough phony? Get it, son?"

"Sure," grinned Ellery; but then the grin faded, and his fork bonged against his plate. "The Burke case," he choked.

His father stared. "The Burke case? What about the Burke case?"

"I knew we were played for suckers, Dad, but till you threw me that puzzle just now, I didn't see how!"

"How?" repeated the Inspector, bewildered.

"Burke didn't commit suicide—*he was murdered*. Take your crime puzzle," said Ellery swiftly. "The Museum of Art alibi and the Flatbush bar alibi might or might not have been false, and only an investigation would tell, but the phone-call-to-the-bookie alibi needs no investigation—it's false on the face of it. No one can dial an exchange like Aqueduct, which starts with the letters AQ, because every phone dial in the United States has one letter of the alphabet missing. *It has no letter Q.*

"And that told me what we'd missed in the Burke setup.

"Dad," cried Ellery, "*that note in Lester Burke's handwriting was a forgery*. If it was a forgery, Burke didn't write it. If Burke didn't write it, he didn't commit suicide—he was murdered. The devil sapped Burke, all right, and placed the unconscious man carefully in the armchair, shot him with his own gun, put Burke's prints on the gun and note, left the forged suicide note on the desk—the kind of note Burke might genuinely have written, a Shakespearian quotation—slipped out with the money and letters, and rejoined his alibi-ing confederates.

"But the fact that the note was a forgery identifies the killer. Ackley is a jewel thief and society impersonator. Chase is a cardsharp. Benson is a confidence man—but he's something else, too. One of his aliases is Phil the Penman—*a tag only a professional forger could have earned!*"

"Yes, but wait, wait," protested Inspector Queen. "But how do you *know* that suicide note was a fake?"

"Benson pulled a boner. Do you remember how he spelled the word 'honor'—spelled it twice—in the quotation?"

"Honor?" The Inspector frowned. "H-o-n-o-r. What's wrong with that, Ellery?"

"Burke was an Englishman, Dad. Had he written that quotation, he'd have spelled 'honor' the way all Englishmen spell it . . . *h-o-n-o-u-r. It had no letter U!*"

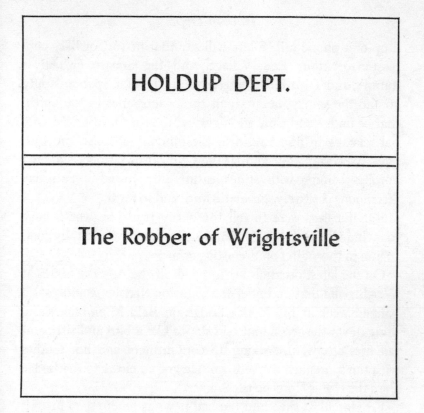

HOLDUP DEPT.

The Robber of Wrightsville

WRIGHTSVILLE IS A New England industrial town famous for nothing, set down in the center of an agricultural county of no particular interest. It was founded by a man named Jezreel Wright in 1701, and after two hundred and fifty-odd years its population is just past ten thousand. Parts of it are crooked and narrow, other parts glare with neon signs, and a great deal of it is downright dingy. In other words, Wrightsville is a very ordinary American town.

But to Ellery it is Shangri-La.

Pressed to explain why he runs off to Wrightsville at the

drop of a phone call, Ellery will say that he sort of likes cob-blestoned, grimy Low Village, and the Square (which is round), and Twin Hill Cemetery and The Hot Spot on Route 16 and the smoky burgundy of the Mahoganies to the north; that he finds Band Concert Night behind the Our Boys Memorial relaxing in direct ratio to the amount of noise and buttered popcorn produced; that the sight of the farmers' starched families coming with stiff pleasure into town on Saturday afternoons positively stimulates him; and so forth.

But if Ellery were to tell the entire truth, he would have to include the fact that Wrightsville has been wonderfully good to him in the matter of interesting crimes.

On the latest occasion he dropped off the Atlantic Stater at Wrightsville Station under the delusion that he would pass a bangup week at Bill York's Lodge on Bald Mountain, skimming down the second-rate ski slopes like a bird and sitting at tall fires afterward, soaking up contentment and hot toddies with the sportsmen of the town. He got no closer to the Lodge than the Hollis Hotel on the Square.

Ed Hotchkiss gave him the bad news as he dumped his skis into Ed's taxi outside the station and turned to churn the large Hotchkiss hand. There wasn't enough snow on Old Baldy this winter, Ed mourned, to make a passable fight for Bill York's six youngsters. But as long as Mr. Queen was in town, there *was* that darned business of Ed's second cousin Mamie and Mamie's boy Delbert . . .

When Ellery had checked into the Hollis, washed up, and come down to the lobby to buy a *Wrightsville Record* at Grover Doodle's cigar stand, he was already half committed to look into the case of young Delbert Hood, who was out on bail awaiting trial for a crime Ed Hotchkiss said his cousin

Mamie said her boy hadn't had a thing in the world to do with.

Certain elements of the affair encouraged the great man's interest. For one thing, the victim of the crime seemed the villain of the piece. For another, Officer Jeep Jorking, one of Chief Dakin's bright young men, was in Wrightsville General Hospital, his left side incased in a cast from the hip down. For a third, everybody in town except Ed Hotchkiss and Mamie Hood Wheeler was convinced that the boy Delbert had done it.

This last by itself was almost enough for Ellery; and by the time he had rooted around among some Wrightsville ladies of his acquaintance, busy at their organizational luncheons at the Hollis and Upham House, and had chewed the fat with Chief Dakin at police headquarters and sundry others, Ellery was ready to go the whole hog.

The background of the case, according to the ladies, was as follows:

Wrightsville had awakened one morning to learn that Anson K. Wheeler was marrying the Widow Hood. This was tantamount to a revolution, for Anse Wheeler was Hill Drive and Mamie Hood was Low Village.

It was not as if Mamie Hood were young and beautiful. She was forty-six if she was a day. Her features were definitely on the common side, and one of the ladies reported that Tessie Lupin, popular operator of the Lower Main Beauty Shop, had never given Mamie Hood so much as a facial, and didn't her complexion look it! As for Mamie's figure, averred the ladies, it was spready around the top and the middle and, when you got right down to it, so to speak, around the bottom, too. She didn't know what a decent foundation garment *was*, apparently.

And there was Anse Wheeler, from one of the old families. The Wheeler mansion on Hill Drive was a showplace. The Wheelers were proud of their name, careful with their money, and properly set in their ways. Anse still drove the Pierce-Arrow which had belonged to his father. They had never streamlined their plumbing. Old Mrs. Wheeler, who wore boned chokers and a gold chest-watch to the day of her death, nevertheless had always insisted on putting up her own pickles. And even though Anson K. Wheeler owned the big farm machinery plant over in the valley near the airport—employing hundreds of people—he conducted his business the way his father had before him, along the most conservative lines, with 1910 bookkeeping methods and Anse personally picking up his plant payroll at the bank every Friday morning.

Anse had been First Selectman twice. He was president of the Wrightsville Historical Society. He was senior vestryman of St. Paul's-in-the-Dingle, with a cold rebuke for those so prone to Low Church lapses as to fail to call the rector "Father" Chichering. His grandfather, General Murdock Wheeler, had been Wrightsville's last surviving veteran of the G.A.R. His first cousin, Uriah Scott ("U.S.") Wheeler, was principal of Gunnery School over in Fyfield and one of Wright County's leading intellectuals.

Anson Wheeler had never married because of his mother. His devotion to ailing Mrs. Wheeler had been a beautiful thing, and when she died at the age of eighty-nine he was like a fish out of water.

That was when *she* got in *her* licks, of course, with her imitation-lady's voice and sugary ways. Anse Wheeler, just about the best catch in town—and Mamie Hood, *his housekeeper*, caught him!

Mamie Hood was not only his housekeeper—a domestic, really—she had a grown child to boot. Delbert had his father's bad blood. There'd always been something queer about Alf Hood, with his radical ideas and his shifty ways. Alf had sent himself through Merrimac U. by stoking furnaces, waiting on table, and even more menial jobs than that; you always felt he'd do anything to make a dollar. When he opened his law office on State Street he might have got along if he'd played his cards right. Louise Glannis was wild about him and wanted to elope. The Glannises and their set would have accepted him in time to keep the town from talking, and he could have made something of himself. What did the fool do? Jilted Louise and married Mamie Broadbeck of Lower Whistling Street! After that, of course, he was through. He never got a single Hill or High Village client—the Glannises saw to that.

So high-and-mighty Alf wound up tramping the streets looking for work. But it was 1931, in the depression, and Charlie Brady was soon picking him up under the influence. Finally Brady caught him in the act of breaking into Logan's Market at three in the morning. He was trying to steal some groceries—picking out the fanciest brands! Charlie took him around to the old jailhouse on Plum Street and the next morning they found him with both wrists slashed. Mamie gave birth the week after the funeral.

Delbert was his father all over again. Mamie hired out for day work, so the boy grew up a typical Low Village street loafer, with no respect for property, and as uppity as Alf ever was. He actually nursed a *grudge* against Wrightsville. Swore he'd "get even" for what they'd "done" to his father!

A boy like that was bound to get into trouble. The Korean war ought to have straightened him out, but he came back in less than a year with a chest wound, louder-mouthed than before. By this time Mamie was the Wheelers' housekeeper, and all Delbert did was sit around the Wheeler kitchen making sarcastic remarks about the Hill families. For Mamie's sake, Anson Wheeler took him into the plant. Delbert lasted just three weeks. One lunch hour Anse caught him making a speech to a large group of working people, ranting about what fools they were to stand for some of the conditions at the plant. Naturally, Anse had to fire him on the spot.

How Anson Wheeler could have married Mamie Hood after *that*, snapped the ladies, was the only mystery in the entire case. Anse asked for it and he got it—two cracks on the skull and the robbery of fifteen thousand of his dollars, and the sooner that horrible boy was sent up to the State Penitentiary where he belonged, the easier they'd all breathe nights.

"I'll take you up the Hill to see Mamie and Del," said Ed Hotchkiss eagerly.

"Wait, Ed," said Ellery. "Who's Del's lawyer?"

"Mort Danzig. He's got his office over his old man's stationery store near the Bijou, on Lower Main."

"I'll walk over to Mort's while you get your cousin Mamie to bring Delbert there. I'd rather talk to them in friendly territory."

"Who says it's friendly?" And, muttering, Ed drove his taxi off at twice the legal speed limit.

"I just don't know, Mr. Queen," said Ben Danzig's balding son worriedly in his plain office above the clatter of Lower Main. "There's an awfully strong circumstantial case against him. And if *I* can't make up my mind about his guilt or innocence . . . I've begged Mamie to get a different lawyer, but she's latched onto me—"

"Who's sitting in the case, Mort?"

"Judge Peter Preston. Of the Hill Prestons," Mort Danzig added grimly. "If Judge Pete hadn't been sick on and off this winter and the calendar crowded, I'd never have been able to delay the trial this long."

"What's your defense?"

Danzig shrugged. "No positive identification. Failure of the money to be found. Negative stuff. What else can I do? The boy's got no alibi—he says he was tramping the woods, alone, around Granjon Falls—he tried to escape afterward, he's responsible for poor Jeep Jorking's being laid up in the hospital, and there's that blamed handkerchief . . ." The young lawyer stared at Ellery hopefully. "Do *you* think Del Hood is innocent?"

"I don't know yet," said Ellery. "Del did me a good turn once on a case, when he was bellhopping at the Hollis, and I remember him as a smart, nice kid. Mort, who went bail for him?"

"Anson Wheeler."

"*Wheeler?*"

"Well, the boy's ma is Anse's wife now, isn't she? You know the cockeyed code these old Hill families live by?"

"But—then why did Wheeler press the charge?"

"That," said Morton F. Danzig dryly, "is another section of said code. *I* don't pretend to understand it. . . . Oh, come in!"

Mamie Hood Wheeler was a plump, sturdy woman who looked like any year's All-American Mother, dressed up for the annual ceremony. She wore a modish hat and a Persian lamb coat which shrieked of newness and Boston. There was nothing Boston could do for her hands, however; they were worked out, in ruins, and beyond repair. (She carried her gloves.) From the state of her eyes, she had been crying since September, and this was January.

If she'd stop crying, Ellery thought, she'd be an attractive woman. What were those women talking about?

"Now, now, Mrs. Wheeler," he said, taking her hands. "I can't promise anything."

"I know you'll get my Del off," she sobbed. She had a soft, surprisingly cultivated, voice. "Thank you, thank you, Mr. Queen!"

"Mom." The tall boy with her was embarrassed. He was lean and burnt-out-looking, with a slow, unhappy smile. "Hello, Mr. Queen. What do you want to bother with me for?"

"Del," said Ellery, looking him in the eye, "did you hold up your stepfather on the Ridge Road last September twenty-first and rob him of his payroll?"

"No, sir. But I don't expect you to believe me."

"No reason why you should," Ellery said cheerfully. "Tell me this, Del: How do you explain that handkerchief?"

"It was planted. I hadn't worn it for weeks—in fact, I thought I'd lost it."

"But he didn't mention it to anybody," said Mort Danzig. "Just to make it harder."

"I tell you I'm being framed, Mr. Danzig!"

"And this, Del," said Ellery. "Why, when Officer Jorking arrested you, did you try to run for it?"

"Because I went chicken. I knew they'd all hang it on me.

It wasn't only the handkerchief. There were all those fights I'd had with old Anse."

"Del," wept his mother, "don't speak about your—about Mr. Wheeler that way. He thinks he's doing the right thing. What we've got to do is convince him—everybody—that you had nothing to do with it."

"What do you want me to do, Mom," cried the tall boy, "kiss his foot for trying to send me to prison? He's had it in for me from the day he caught me explaining to some of his plant workers what suckers they are. I should have cleared out then!"

"You've been out on bail for months," remarked Ellery. "Why haven't you cleared out while you've had the chance?"

The boy flushed. "I'm not that big a rat, with him putting up the bail. Besides, my mother still has to live in this one-horse town. The only thing I'm sorry about is that I lost my head when Jeep Jorking tried to pull me in."

"And you're still living in your stepfather's house, Del?"

"It's my mother's house now, too, isn't it?" Delbert said defiantly. "She's got some rights as his wife."

"Del," moaned Mamie.

"But isn't it awkward, Del? For you as well as for Mr. Wheeler?"

"We just ignore each other."

"Seems to me," said Ellery, "your stepfather's been awfully decent about several phases of this affair."

"All right!" shouted Delbert Hood. "I'll give him my Purple Heart!"

That was one of the things Ellery liked about this case. The villain was something of a saint and the young hero could have used a timely kick in the pants.

"Well, Delbert, there's only one way to get you out of this

hole. If you're innocent, somebody else is guilty. Take your
mom home and stay there with her. You'll hear from me."

Ellery crossed the Square to the Wrightsville National Bank
and asked to see its president, Wolfert Van Horn.

Old Wolf hadn't changed. He merely looked older, scratch-
ier, and more wolfish. He eyed Ellery's hand as if it were
diseased and sat back to click his dentures carnivorously.

"You'll get no cooperation from me, Queen," said Wrightsville's leading banker in his knifelike voice. "That boy's guilty
and Anse Wheeler is one of my bank's best customers. Would
you like to open an account?"

"Now, Wolfert," said Ellery soothingly, "all I'm trying to do
is pick up the facts of a business that happened almost five
months ago. Tell me how Anson Wheeler's regular payroll day
happened to be changed after so many years."

"Nothing to tell," said Wolfert Van Horn with a snarl of
sheer hatred. "Tellers always made up Anse's payroll Thursday late afternoon, and first thing Friday morning Anse would
pick it up at the bank here on his way to the plant. One Friday
morning, middle of last September, a man with a handkerchief
over his face tried to hold him up on the Ridge Road. Anse got
away by stepping on the gas. So the next week—"

"Time," murmured Ellery. "As a result of the near holdup,
Mr. Wheeler called a council of war that same evening at his
home. Who were actually present at that meeting—in his
study, I believe?"

"Anse Wheeler, Mamie, Chief Dakin, me, and my head
cashier, Olin Keckley."

"Not Delbert Hood, then."

"He wasn't in the study, no. But he was in the living room

reading a pile of comic books, and the transom over the door between was wide open. Couldn't have helped but hear the whole thing."

"Delbert was still in the living room when the conference broke up and you left?"

"He was," said Wolfert, beginning to enjoy himself, "and I'm going to say so on the witness stand under oath."

"At this meeting, it was decided that, unless the masked man were picked up beforehand, the next week Keckley would make up the Wheeler payroll on Wednesday instead of Thursday, and on Wednesday evening he, Keckley, would secretly take the payroll to your home. Mr. Wheeler was to pick it up at your house Thursday morning on his way to the plant. And all this was to be kept top-secret among those present. Is that right, Wolfert?"

"I know what you're after," grinned Van Horn, "but it wasn't *my* handkerchief that's Exhibit Number One in this case."

"Tell me: Whose suggestion was it that the payroll day be advanced from Friday to Thursday?"

Wolfert started. "What difference does that make?" he demanded suspiciously. "I don't remember, anyhow!"

"Could we have Olin Keckley in here?"

Van Horn's head cashier was a gaunt gray man with a tic and a cringing look. In the days when John F. Wright had owned the bank, Ellery recalled, Keckley had been a pleasant fellow with a forthright eye.

"The suggestion about changing the day?" the cashier repeated, glancing quickly at Wolfert Van Horn. The banker looked bland. "Why, I'm sure I don't remember, Mr. Queen." Wolfert frowned. "Unless," Keckley hurried on, "unless it was

me. Yes, I think—in fact, I'm sure it was me made the suggestion."

"Why, Olin, I think it was," said his employer.

"Clever of you, Mr. Keckley," said Ellery. Chief Dakin
had told him the suggestion originated with Wolfert Van
Horn. "And the following Wednesday night you dropped the
Wheeler payroll off at Mr. Van Horn's house, as planned?"

"Yes, sir."

"The payroll was in the customary canvas bag?"

"Well, no, sir. We figured that since the whole idea was
to fool the robber, we ought to wrap the payroll in paper, like
an ordinary package. In case," Keckley said earnestly, "the robber was watching the bank, or something like that."

"What kind of paper?"

"Plain brown wrapping paper."

"Sealed?"

"With adhesive paper tape, yes, sir."

"I take it, Mr. Keckley, you didn't discuss the new plan with
anyone at all?"

"No, sir! I didn't even let the other tellers see me make up
the Wheeler payroll that Wednesday afternoon."

"And I suppose you didn't give any information away, Wolfert," said Ellery when the cashier, perspiring, had fled. "I
know, I know; don't bother. What time that Thursday morning
did Anson Wheeler pick the payroll up at your house?"

"Quarter past seven."

"That early?" Ellery sat up. "And he was going directly to
the Ridge Road, to his plant?"

"The plant's work day starts eight o'clock."

"While the Wrightsville National Bank," murmured Ellery,

"doesn't open its doors till nine-thirty." He rose suddenly. "Be seeing you, Wolfert!"

Ellery had Ed Hotchkiss drive him up to Hill Valley. At the point where Shingle Street ends and Route 478A turns east to Twin Hill-in-the-Beeches, the Ridge Road begins, bearing north around the heavily forested hills above Wrightsville and then due west into the Valley.

Ed slowed his taxi down. "This is where the dirty work was done, Mr. Queen. Nothing here but the road and woods, y'see—"

"We'll nose around the scene of the foul deed in due course, Edward. First let's talk to Anse Wheeler."

The Wheeler Company occupied a long low building of blackened brick not far from Wrightsville Airport. It was as ugly a factory as the old machine shop in Low Village, which was Ellery's standard frame of reference. Inside, the building was poorly lighted and ventilated, the floors sagged alarmingly under the weight of the heavy machinery, generations of dirt crusted the walls, and the workmen labored in silence. Ellery, who had begun to like Anson Wheeler, decided to dislike him all over again.

He found the owner in a bare, chilly office of scarified golden oak. Wheeler was a tense-looking man of middle age and height, with eyes as pale as his cheeks. His highpitched voice had a chronic note of resentment in it, almost a whine.

"I know, I know what you're here for, Mr. Queen," he said bitterly. "Van Horn's already phoned me. Well, I consider myself a fair man. I won't have you think I'm persecuting him. But I tell you the boy did it. If I weren't convinced, do you think I'd press this case? I'm—I'm very fond of Mrs. Wheeler. But she's got to see Delbert as he really is. A troublemaker, a thief! It's not the money, Mr. Queen. It's . . . *him.*"

"But suppose, Mr. Wheeler, you found out that Del didn't do it?"

"I'd be a very happy man," said Anse Wheeler with a groan. Then his thin lips tightened. "But he did."

"That first time—the unsuccessful attempt. Did you get a good look at the masked man before you got away?"

"Well, he was sort of tall, and thin. There was a silk-looking handkerchief over his face. I was too excited to notice anything else. But later, looking back, I saw that it must have been Delbert."

"He was pointing a gun, I believe?"

"Yes. The boy has a gun. He brought one back with him from Korea."

"He made no attempt to fire after you as you stepped on the gas?"

"I don't know. They didn't find any bullet holes in the car. I almost ran him down. He jumped into a bush."

"You realize, of course, Mr. Wheeler, that it might have been anybody tall and thin . . ."

"You think I'm pinning it on him!" cried Anse Wheeler. "Well, how about that handkerchief? The next Thursday?"

"Tell me about it, Mr. Wheeler," said Ellery sympathetically.

"I picked up my payroll at Wolfert's house early that morning and took the Ridge Road as usual." Wheeler's high voice climbed higher. "There, at almost the same spot as the Friday morning before, was a tree across the road. I came on it so

unexpectedly around the bend, all I could think to do was jam
on my brakes, grab the package of money, and try to run for
it . . . He—he hit me. As I got out of my car."

"Del hit you, Mr. Wheeler?" murmured Ellery.

"I didn't actually see him, no. My back was to him. But wait!
The whack on my head dazed me only for a second or two—
he must have missed where he was aiming. I tried to fight him."
Wheeler's pale eyes flashed fire suddenly. "He's a strong boy
and he's been in the Army—oh, he knew how to get me! He
crooked his arm around my throat from behind, and I was
helpless. I reached up and tried to claw at his face. I felt something silky in my fingers and then he hit me on the back of
the head again. Next thing I knew Officer Jorking was reviving
me. The money was gone, but I'd held on to the handkerchief.
It was Delbert's."

"You're positive," said Ellery, "it was his."

"Had his initials on it! I'd given him that silk pocket handkerchief when I married his mother. I outfitted that boy from
head to foot . . . !"

Ellery left Anson K. Wheeler in his grimy office, tight face
bloodless and long fingers feeling the back of his head.

Officer Jorking lay in the men's ward at Wrightsville General Hospital, munching disgustedly at a winter apple. His left
leg and thigh were buried to the hip in a bulky cast, and he
was lying in a maze of traction apparatus.

"I feel like some screwball's invention," said the young
policeman out of a deep gloom. "And stuck in this contraption
since last September! If they don't give that kid ten years, Mr.
Queen, I'll personally break his neck."

"Tough all around, Jeep," mourned Ellery, sitting down beside the hospital bed. "How did it happen?"

Young Jorking spat out an apple pip. "The Ridge Road's part of my beat—I cover the whole district north of town. When Mr. Wheeler was almost held up that first time, Chief Dakin ordered me to keep my eye on him without letting on. So when Wheeler picked up his payroll that morning at Van Horn's on North Hill Drive, I was tailing his Pierce in my prowl car.

"He turned into Ridge Road, me staying far enough back so I won't scare off the robber if he should give it another try. That's how the kid got away from me. I didn't come around the bend of the road till it was all over. Wheeler was stretched out cold, blood streaming from his head, and a skinny tall figure was just diving into the woods to the east of the road."

"To the *east*."

"Yes, sir. I fired a couple of snap shots in his direction, but I didn't hit anything, and by the time I'd pulled up where he'd gone for cover, there wasn't a sign of him. So I reported to headquarters on my two-way radio and took care of Mr. Wheeler. He wasn't dead, wasn't even hurt bad.

"The first thing I spotted was that silk handkerchief in his hand with the initials *D. H.* Every buck in town knew that silk handkerchief—it was the first one young Del'd ever owned, and he kept showing it off—so I knew right away who it had been."

"How did he break your hip?" asked Ellery.

"I broke it going after him." The young officer spat out another pip. "Del walked into the house quite a while after I got Mr. Wheeler home and was fixing his head. The kid was sort of scratched up and his clothes were full of bits of twig and thorn. He said he'd been tramping through the woods. I told him what happened, showed him his hanky, and said I'd have to pull him in. Darned if he didn't take off!—jumped clean through a window. I chased him along the edge of that ravine behind the Wheeler house, and that's how I came to bust my hip. Tripped over a root and fell smack into the ravine. It's a wonder I didn't break my back. . . . It was Del packed me out of there. Seems he saw me tumble in and decided to turn Boy Scout."

Young Jorking scowled at his mummified left foot and flung the apple core at it. "Ah, it's a mixed-up kind of case, Mr. Queen. I wish I didn't have to testify."

So then Ellery went over to police headquarters and sat down in Chief Dakin's swivel chair near the picture of J. Edgar Hoover, and he said, "Mind if I mull over this for a while, old pal?"

"Mull away," grunted Dakin. The chief stood at his window studying State Street.

Finally Ellery said, "My muller seems out of order. Did you consider any other possibilities, Dakin?"

"Like fury," said the chief of police, not unkindly. "But who would you have me pin it on? The only other ones who knew about that switch in payroll days were Wheeler himself, Mamie, Wolfert Van Horn, and Olin Keckley.

"Wolf Van Horn might have done it, sure, if there were a million or two involved. But I can't see him risking the Pen at his age for a measly fifteen thousand—not with all the money he's got. Keckley? A man like Olin might help himself from the till under certain circumstances, but armed robbery? masks? hitting folks over the head? jumping into bushes?" The chief shook his head. "Not Olin. He'd faint dead away first."

"Then one of them blabbed!"

"Could be. Only they all say they didn't."

"Damn! I'd like to get that boy off." Ellery gnawed a knuckle. "About the payroll, Dakin. You never found any part of it, hm?"

"Nary a dime."

"Where'd you look?"

"We searched the Wheeler house and grounds, and just about every other place in and out of town young Del's known to hang around. He's got it hid away somewhere, of course. Probably hid it right after the holdup."

"Did you search the woods?"

"Near the scene, on the theory that the robber might have dropped it when Jorking chased him, or hid it as part of a plan? Yep," said Chief Dakin, "we searched those woods east of the road with a fine-tooth comb, Mr. Queen."

"Just east of the road?"

Dakin stared. "That's the direction the robber took when he lit out."

"But why not west, too? He might have doubled back across the road somewhere out of Jeep's view!"

Dakin shook his head. "You're wasting your time, Mr. Queen. Supposing you even found the money. That'd be fine for Anse Wheeler, but how would it help get young Del off?"

"It's a loose end," said Ellery irritably. "You never know how a loose end ties in, Dakin. And anyway, I've covered everything else. Come on, you're going to search with me."

They found the stolen Wheeler payroll in the woods not fifty yards west of the Ridge Road, on a due line from the spot where Anse Wheeler had been held up the preceding September.

Chief Dakin was chagrined. "I feel like a dummy!"

"Needn't," said Ellery, intent, on his knees. "Last fall these woods were in full foliage, and to have found anything like this would have constituted an act of God. In January, with the trees stripped bare and the ground clear, it's a different boiler of bass."

The package of money had been buried in a shallow pit at the base of a tree. But rains and winds had torn away the thin covering of dirt and leafmold, and both men had spotted the package at the same time, bulging soddenly out of the earth.

Nature had been unkind to Anson Wheeler's payroll. The brown paper in which it was wrapped had disintegrated under the action of soil and elements. Small animals and birds had evidently gnawed at rotting, mildewed, moldy bills. Insects had contributed to the wreckage. Most of the paper money was in unrecognizable, fused lumps and shreds.

"If there's two thousand dollars in salvage left, *including* the silver," muttered Wrightsville's chief of police, "Anse is in luck. Only there ain't."

"It was that awfully hot Indian summer and this mild winter," murmured Ellery. "Most of the damage was done before the ground hardened." Ellery got to his feet. "Fortunately."

"For who?"

"For Del Hood. This mass of corruption is going to keep young Delbert out of quad."

"What!"

"Up to now I've only hoped the boy was innocent. Now I know it."

Chief Dakin stared at him. Then, bewilderedly, he squatted

to examine the remains of the payroll, as if he had missed a clue buried in it somewhere.

"But I don't see—!"

"Later, Dakin. Right now we'd better use my topcoat to gather this filth up in. It's evidence!"

And when everyone was arranged to Ellery's satisfaction, he looked about him and he said, "This one has the beautiful merit of simplicity.

"Look.

"Robber assaults Mr. Wheeler on the Ridge Road, snatches the payroll in its paper wrappings, and shortly thereafter buries the package in a very shallow pit in the woods not fifty yards from the scene of the robbery. This is last September I'm talking about.

"Now a robber who buries his loot immediately after he's stolen it either intends it as a temporary cache—till the first hue and cry blows over—or as a long-term hiding place . . . till the case is practically forgotten, say, or till he's taken a world cruise, or served a prison term.

"Did our robber mean that hole in the woods to be the hiding place of his loot for a short time, or a long time?

"For a short time," said Ellery, answering himself, "obviously. No robber in his right mind would take fifteen thousand dollars in paper money, wrapped in paper wrappings, and bury it for any length of time. If he had the sense he was born with he'd know what he'd find when he came back—what, in fact, Chief Dakin and I did find—a soggy, eaten-up, chewed-away, soil-eroded, disintegrated wad of valueless pulp. For a long-time burial, he'd have provided himself with a weather-resist-

ant, strong container of some sort, of metal or even of heavy
wood.

"Our robber, then, had nothing of the sort in mind. By
burying the payroll in its perishable paper wrappings—in a
shallow hole—he tells us that he intended it to lie there for a
very short time. Perhaps only for hours, or at the most, days.

"As it turns out, *he left it there for almost five months—*
until, as you see, it was practically destroyed. I ask the reasonable question: Why, after planning to retrieve it in a short
time, did he leave it there to rot? Certainly at some period in
the past five months it must have been perfectly safe for him
to dig it up. In fact, he would have been safe any time after the
first few days. Nobody's been shadowed in this case—not even
Del, out on bail. And the spot is a lonely one, well off the
road in the woods. So again I ask: Why didn't the robber come
back for his loot? To spend it, or to transfer it to another hiding place, or to repackage it if for no other reason?"

Ellery grinned without much humor. He said simply: "If he
didn't come back for the payroll when there was every reason
for him to do so, and no risk, logically it can only have been
because he couldn't come back. And that's why I've had you
wheeled into this private room," Ellery said, turning to the
young policeman trussed up on the hospital bed, "so you could
face the man you've victimized and the woman you've cruci-
fied and the boy you've tried to throw to the dogs, Jeep—yes,
and the honest cop who trained you and trusted you and who's
looking at you now and seeing you, I'm sure, really for the first
time.

"You're the only one of those involved, Jorking, who physically could not get back to that cache in the woods.

"You learned about the change in the payroll day through Chief Dakin, who assigned you the job of tailing Mr. Wheeler in your prowl car. But you didn't tail Mr. Wheeler in your prowl car that morning, Jorking—you were already on your selected site, as you had been the week before, lurking behind your ambush, your police car hidden off the road somewhere.

"You assaulted Mr. Wheeler from behind and you saw to it that that silk handkerchief of Del's—explaining how Del 'lost' it—remained in Mr. Wheeler's grip. If he hadn't ripped it off your face you would have left it in or near his hand. And while he was still unconscious, you darted into the woods and hastily buried the package of money—because you were playing two roles at the moment and time was precious just then—intending to come back for it later in the day, or the next day, when the coast would be clear. Only on taking Mr. Wheeler back to his home and solemnly arresting Delbert for the crime you had committed, the boy bolted, you chased him, you broke your hip, and they rushed you to the hospital where you've been immobilized in a cast ever since! You're not only a thief, Jeep, you're a disgrace to an undervalued profession, and I'm going to hang around in Wrightsville long enough to see you immobilized in the clink."

When Ellery turned from the frozen man in the bed, he realized that he was—in a queer sense—quite alone. Chief Dakin was facing the wall. Mamie Hood Wheeler sat crying joyfully in a sphere of her own. And above her Anse Wheeler, so pale with excitement that he was sky-blue, thumped Del Hood repeatedly on the chest, and Del Hood, with wild friendliness, was giving his stepfather back thump for thump.

So Ellery went away, quietly.

SWINDLE DEPT.

Double Your Money

IF THEODORE F. GROOSS HAD DECIDED to run for Mayor of New York, he would have carried all of the West Eighties between the park and the river by a record plurality, and possibly—in time—the rest of the city as well. Fortunately for the traditional parties, however, Grooss's forte was not politics but finance. He was the people's champion of sound money in the era of inflation. In a day when the dollar bought little more than fifty cents' worth of anything, Grooss's genius found a way to restore it to its par excellence. His solution was wonderful: He made each dollar, like the ameba, reproduce itself.

For this feat, which he performed regularly for the benefit of all comers, he was known to some of his fervid constituents as "the Wizard of Amsterdam Avenue," but most of them called him, with homely grandeur, "Double-Your-Money" Grooss.

What Ellery called him is not to be printed.

Ellery first heard about Theodore F. Grooss from Mr. Joe Belcassazzi, head of the maintenance department of the three-story brownstone on West Eighty-seventh Street where the Queens reside. Mr. Belcassazzi, whose only investments heretofore had been in *pasta* for his large and unappeasable family, stopped wrestling a can of furnace ashes on the sidewalk to expound to the attentive Mr. Queen the glory that was Grooss. Mr. Belcassazzi had a normally hangdog eye, but it was on fire with joy this morning.

"He's take twelve dollar twenty-five cents of my insurance money," cried Mr. Belcassazzi, "and in three months he give me back twenty-four dollars and fifty cents! *Madre!* You got a few bucks, Mr. Queen, you give 'em to the Wizza. Everybody's doin' it."

Mr. Queen forgot what had brought him out into the sunshine. He went round the corner to Amsterdam Avenue and stopped in here and there. Everybody was indeed doing it. Mr. Rickhardt, the butcher of Frank's Fancy Market, had already realized one hundred percent on each of two investments with Wizard Grooss, and he was weighing a third with the critical air of a member of the Stock Exchange. The widowed Mrs. Cahn of the Delicious Bakery was excitedly contemplating her second. Old Mr. Patterson of the silver shop stopped polishing a pair of antique candlesticks long enough to quaver the admission that he, too, was a satisfied client of Theodore F.

Grooss's. And so it went, up and down and on both sides of the Avenue. And, Ellery suspected, in the cross streets, too.

"He's even got the school kids giving him their lunch money," Ellery protested to his father that night. "The whole neighborhood's involved, Dad. Guaranteeing to double their money in three months! Can't you do something about the fellow?"

"First I hear about him," said Inspector Queen thoughtfully. "Certainly the D. A.'s office hasn't had any complaints."

"Because he's still paying off, setting up the kill. The oldest swindle in the book!" Ellery waved his long arms menacingly. "Grooss isn't 'investing' their money. He's simply paying off investors of three months ago out of the money he's accepting today. You know how this sort of thing mushrooms once the word gets round, Dad. For each payoff he gets a dozen new suckers—he's always miles ahead of the game. The only thing is, one of these days he's going to take an unannounced vacation with a trunkful of his client's undoubled dough."

"I'll put the D. A.'s office onto him, Ellery."

"I can't wait that long! Charlie Felipez just borrowed a hundred dollars from a loan company to give to Grooss." Charlie Felipez was the war amputee who ran a newsstand in the neighborhood. "Others are pulling the same foolish stunt. Let's throw a scare into this operator, Dad. Maybe we can bluff him into doing something stupid."

The Inspector looked interested. "Anything in mind?"

"The full treatment. What are you the whitehaired boy of Center Street for?"

At 8:15 the next morning, with all arrangements made, the Queens and Sergeant Thomas Velie of the Inspector's staff called on the Wizard of Amsterdam Avenue. Early as it was, the seventh-floor corridor of the office building was packed wall to wall. Ellery winced. There was young Minnie Bender, who supported a spastic child by her earnings at the steam table of the 89th St. Cafeteria; he recognized two elderly women who clerked in Crawford's Five-and-Ten, the young boy from Harlem who shined shoes in the barbershop, the ex-refugee corned-beef-and-pastrami man of Garbitsch's Delicatessen, the bartender of Haenigsen's Grill, the one with the two sons in Korea—wherever Ellery looked he spied familiar faces, familiar hands clutching bills of low denominations. The pressure of the crowd had burst the lock of the front door of Grooss's office and what looked like an anteroom was jammed with humanity. Even with Sergeant Velie running interference, the Queens had to claw their way into the outer office.

"Quit your shoving!"

"We were here first!"

"Who do they think they are?"

"Where," roared the Inspector over the hubbub, "is this Theodore F. Grooss?"

"He ain't in yet."

"He opens for business nine o'clock."

"Velie! Everybody outside."

In a few minutes the anteroom was clear and the Sergeant's mammoth back shadowed the pebbled glass of the front door from the hall. A few alarmed voices were audible, but they were soon lost in the goodnatured heckling of the crowd.

A door in the side wall of the anteroom was giltlettered *T. F. Grooss, Private.* Ellery tried it. It was locked.

The Queens sat down on a wooden bench in the cheaply furnished office, and they waited.

At 8:35 a surflike roar from outside brought them to their feet. The next moment the corridor door flew open and a rosy-cheeked man, smiling and waving like a home-coming hero, skipped under one of Sergeant Velie's outspread arms into the anteroom. The Sergeant slammed the door and the cries of joy turned to groans.

"Good morning, gentlemen," said Double-Your-Money Grooss briskly. "That man out there says you're waiting to see me on important business. What can I do for you?" As he spoke, Grooss began to pick up his morning mail, which the feet of the crowd had trampled and scattered. He was a stout, fatherly-looking gentleman with a military gray mustache, a glistening bald head, a mealy voice, and the richly subdued garb of an elder statesman. "Gracious, they must have broken in again. Do you know, I've had this lock fixed twice this week?"

Inspector Queen looked unimpressed. He produced his shield and said mildly, "Inspector, police headquarters. This is Ellery Queen."

"Oh . . . yes. Some of my oldest clients are members of the Finest," said Grooss, beaming. "Thinking of investing, gentlemen?"

"Well, it's a fact, Mr. Grooss," said Ellery, "we're here to explore the subject with you . . . exhaustively."

"Ah. Certainly! If you'll give me a few minutes to go through my mail . . ." Grooss bustled to the door of his private office, fumbling with a key on a chain.

"Fifteen minutes," said Ellery. "No more."

"And then," added Inspector Queen, showing his denture, "I've got a little something for you, Mr. Grooss." His palm touched his breast pocket, gently.

But the Wizard's cheeks did not lose their rosy color. He merely nodded, a bit absently, unlocked his office door, went in, and closed the door behind him.

"An old hand," muttered the Inspector. "It's not going to work, son."

"You never can tell," said Ellery, glancing at his watch; and he sat down and lit a cigaret. All exits from the building were now guarded by blue coats, under orders not to let anyone leave. If Grooss lost his head . . .

Thirteen minutes later there was another commotion outside. Inspector Queen sprang to the corridor and flung it open. A thin pale little man with dank brown hair and a cadaverous face screwed into an expression of chronic worry was dangling from Sergeant Velie's fist.

"But I tell you I work here!" wailed the little man. "I'm Albert Crocker, the office assistant. Please let me in. Mr. Grooss will be mad—I'm late—"

"Let him in, Velie." The Inspector dismissed the clerk with a glance. Grooss's generosity in making money apparently did not extend to his clerk; Crocker was seedily dressed and he looked in need of a good breakfast. "Grooss is in his private office, Crocker. Better get him out here."

"Is—something wrong, sir?" There was sweat on the man's upper lip.

"Tell him," said Ellery, "his time is up."

The clerk's nervousness mounted. He hurried to the door marked *Private*, opened it, and slipped into his employer's office.

"Crocker may come in handy," murmured Ellery.

"Uh-huh. We'll give him an audition. I'll bet he sings! What's the matter, Crocker?"

The miserable clerk was in the doorway, more worried-looking than before. "Did you say Mr. Grooss was in here, sir?"

"He's *not?*" cried the Inspector; and with a grin of triumph he pushed Crocker aside and darted into the inner office.

It was a long narrow dingy room, spartanly furnished—a flat-top desk, two wooden chairs, a few card-index drawers, a clothestree. The room was empty.

"We bluffed him into trying a runout!" chortled the Inspector. "They'll grab him at one of the street exits with a suitcase full of cash—"

"Maybe not," said Ellery in a peculiar voice.

"What did you say, son?"

"If Grooss was able to get out of this room, Dad, a guarded street exit isn't necessarily going to stop him."

His father stared.

"Take a look around. A good look."

The Inspector's happiness congealed. He saw now that there were only two exits from Grooss's private office: the doorway to the anteroom in which the Queens had been waiting from the moment Grooss entered his office, and the window overlooking Amsterdam Avenue seven floors below. And while the usual narrow ledge ran along outside the window, the window catch was securely fastened *on the inside*.

A single door, under observation every instant; a single window, locked on the inside. And no hiding place anywhere in the room large enough to conceal a small monkey!

"Did they say," said Inspector Queen feebly, "wizard?"

For the next eternity Ellery gave a credible imitation of a man working out an abstruse problem in Bedlam. The mob swirled all about the desk at which he sat in the inner office, shrieking for their hard-earned money and the blood of the vanished Wizard. They would have torn poor Crocker into small pieces if Sergeant Velie had not straddled him and made threatening gestures with his police revolver. The Sergeant kept yelling for reinforcements. At last they came—Inspector Queen and six uniformed men, looking dazed. The policemen began struggling with the people and the Inspector rammed his way to the desk and glared down at his cogitating son.

"*Ellery!*"

Ellery looked up. "Oh. Nothing, Dad?"

"No!" snarled the Inspector. "The men swear on the memory of their mothers that they didn't let Grooss—or anyone else!—out of the building. But where is he? And how in thunder did he get out of this room?"

"Yeah, where is he?" screamed a woman's voice.

"And where's our dough?" howled a man from a bluecoat's grasp.

Ellery climbed onto the Wizard's desk. "If you'll quiet down, I'll answer all your questions!" he shouted. The mob stilled instantly. "Grooss is a smart crook. He had his getaway planned for any emergency. When he saw an inspector of police he stepped into this private office and closed that door. There are only two exits from this room, the doorway to that outer office where Inspector Queen and I were waiting for him, and the window there overlooking Amsterdam Avenue. Since we can testify that Grooss didn't escape through the outer office, he could only have left through the window. Outside the window there's a narrow ledge, and he inched along that—"

"Through the *window?*" muttered the Inspector. "But son, the window's locked on the inside!"

"As I say," said Ellery, "Grooss inched along the ledge to *the window of the office next door,* an office which he undoubtedly rented long ago for just such a purpose. From the next-door office, carrying his loot, he let himself out up the corridor into the crowd. Then he must have tried to leave the building, but when he saw that police were posted at every exit and that he couldn't get out without being searched, he had to think of something else.

"He saw right away that his big problem was to hide the money until the heat was off and he could sneak it away. Where could he hide it? Obviously, in the prepared office next door, the office he was renting, unknown to anyone, under another name. But for the money to be safe in that office, we mustn't suspect that the office had any connection with Theodore F. Grooss. How could he keep us away from there? Well, he'd got to it by way of this window . . . and at the time he climbed out of this window onto the ledge he obviously had left the window unlocked. If he could *lock* the window, he figured we'd never think of it as his means of escape. So Grooss came back *here,* to his private office, locked the window on the inside—"

"Wait, wait," groaned the Inspector. "What d'ye mean he came back *here?* To do that he'd have had to pass you and me in that anteroom—"

"Exactly," said Ellery.

"But the only one who passed the two of us in the anteroom was . . . Crocker . . ."

"Yes, Crocker," said Ellery. "Crocker walked into this office from the anteroom, ostensibly to send Grooss out to us—but actually to lock the window. Crocker, my friends, is Theodore F. Grooss without the body padding, with the bald wig and mustache and the high coloring and the cotton mouth wads removed—and a quick change of clothes which he's had planted all along in the hideaway office next door—"

Ellery went on to explain that the people's money and Grooss's discarded disguise would be found in the office next door, but nobody heard him, since the Inspector had already darted through the crowd and the crowd, with a whoop, ran after him through the anteroom into the corridor. The thin little man between Sergeant Velie's legs made a sudden vicious gesture and the Sergeant toppled, doubled up. Crocker-Grooss dashed through the anteroom pursued by Ellery's roar.

The little man stopped in the doorway, and this time there was no blood in his face at all. For the people had turned and at sight of him, as one man, they fell silent and opened their arms.

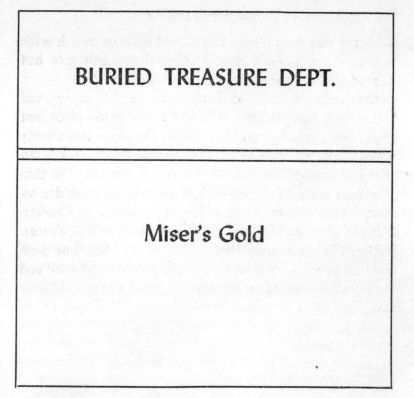

BURIED TREASURE DEPT.

Miser's Gold

It is DOUBTFUL if the chronicler of Baghdad-on-the-Subway ever produced a more wonderful entertainment than the tale of Uncle Malachi. The atmosphere is rich and twisted, the subject likewise, and the story full of sentiment and irony. It even has a surprise ending.

Uncle Malachi was born, he lived, and he died under the rusty shadows of the Third Avenue El. Because he was a pawnbroker and owned the rickety, peeling old building in which he worked and lived, he was said to be Wealthy. Because he was an old crosspatch who distrusted banks and lived like a

mouse, he was said to be a Miser. And since his one notable
passion was the collecting of books—not rare books, or first
editions, or books in perfect condition, but any books in any
condition—he was said to be Queer.

It was all true—he was rich, he was a miser, and he was
queer; but there was more to it than that. His riches came
from selling real estate—Manhattan real estate—which his
great-grandfather had bought; he was a miser, because all
pawnbrokers are born accumulators; and his queerness lay not
in collecting books but in reading them.

Books swarmed like honey bees over his pawnshop and living quarters upstairs, which consisted of two impossibly clut-
tered cubbyholes. Here under jackets of dust could be found
the collected works of such as Dumas, Scott, Cooper, Dickens,
Poe, Stevenson, Kipling, Conrad, Twain, O. Henry, Doyle,
Wells, Jack London—wholesale reading in low-cost lots; and
Malachi devoted every moment he could spare from his shop
to peering through wavering gaslight at the written treasures
of the world. As he aged and eyesight withered, the tempo of
his reading increased; for old Malachi had set himself the fine
labor of reading every famous book ever printed, beginning
with the more exciting ones. A magnificent lunacy, which
went with his spidery mind and mystifying sense of humor—
he was always grinning, chuckling, or laughing, although no
one ever knew what the joke was.

Uncle Malachi's clients were fond of saying that the old
miser had no heart, which was a slander. He had a heart—as
Dr. Ben Bernard, whose shingle drooped two doors up the
street, was prepared to testify—one of the worst hearts, Dr.
Ben said, in his experience, a valvular monstrosity and black

as the devil's. But Uncle Malachi only cackled, "You're a fool, Doctor!" Dr. Ben retorted with a sigh that if he were not a fool he would not be practicing medicine on Third Avenue, and he continued to treat the old pawnbroker as if his monthly bills were honored.

As for Eve Warren, she came into Uncle Malachi's life the way most people did. Eve was struggling to keep her little greeting-card shop and circulating library across the street from the hot clutches of her creditors, so she became one of Malachi's clients. When his eyes failed, she felt a stern duty; there were few enough booklovers in the world. So she began dropping in on him after closing her shop, and she would read to him. At first he was suspicious; but when he saw that she was a fool like Dr. Ben, old Malachi grinned, and after that he would even offer her with antique ceremony a cup of strong hot water which he alleged was tea.

Uncle Malachi's black heart cut its last caper one evening while Eve was reading *Treasure Island* to him. She looked up from Black Dog's wound and Dr. Livesey's lancet to find the pawnbroker on the floor, his head between two heaps of books, eyes popping and face blue-twisted.

"Lawyer. . . witnesses. . . will. . ."

Frankie Pagluighi, who was serving his first clerkship in a Murray Hill law office, was holding forth on the stoop next door to a group of neighbors on the latest Supreme Court decision; Eve screamed to him what was wanted and raced up the street to Dr. Ben's. By the time she and the young doctor got back, Uncle Malachi's head was resting on a red buckram set of Richard Harding Davis, and Attorney Pagluighi was kneeling by his side, writing frantically.

". . . all my property, real and personal . . . including my hidden cash . . . equally between the only human beings . . . who have ever shown me Christian charity. . . ."

Dr. Ben looked up at Eve and shook his head sadly.

". . . Eve Warren and Dr. Ben Bernard."

"Oh!" said Eve; and then she burst into tears.

Grocer Swendssen, Patrolman Pat Curlihy, and Joe Littman of the drygoods store signed as witnesses, and then Frankie Pagluighi bent over the gasping man and said loudly, "This hidden cash you specify. How much does it amount to?" Old Malachi worked his blue lips, but nothing came out. "Five thousand? Ten thousand?"

"Four million." He managed a whisper. "In ten-thousand-dollar bills."

"Million." The young lawyer swallowed. "Four *million?* Dollars? Where? Where is it? Where did you hide it? Mr. Malachi!"

Uncle Malachi tried to speak.

"*Is it in this building?*"

"Yes," said the old man in a suddenly clear voice. "Yes. It's in—"

But then he came to attention and looked far beyond them, and after a while Dr. Ben said he was dead.

Ellery came into the case not only because puzzles were his caviar, but also because it was clear as an aspic that his two callers were hopelessly gone on each other. Love and buried treasure—who could resist such a dish?

"You're sure it's really four million dollars and not four hundred figments of the old man's imagination, Dr. Bernard?"

But Dr. Ben reassured him. In the pawnshop safe had

been found a ledger listing the serial numbers of the ten-thousand-dollar bills, which various banks had confirmed. And Eve said Uncle Malachi had often made slyly mysterious remarks to her about his "cache of cash"—he was fond of puns and tricks, she said—defying anyone to find it, even though he had hidden it "on the premises." And the fact was she and Dr. Ben had gone over the little building from basement to roof, inside and out, and had found nothing but cobwebs and vermin. It was not a total loss, Eve admitted with a blush, for they had become engaged while digging up the cellar, under the sponsorship of an indignant rat which had sent her howling into Dr. Ben's arms.

"Well, well, we'll see about this," said Ellery delightedly; and he went right back to Third Avenue with them.

Sixteen hours later he sank into Uncle Malachi's only chair, a betasseled red-plush refugee from some Victorian town house, and nibbled his thumb. Eve perched disconsolately on Uncle Malachi's bed, and Dr. Ben sat on a pile of books, wedged between The Works of Bret Harte and The Complete Novels of Wilkie Collins. And the gas jet flamed and danced.

"It isn't as if," said Ellery about an hour later, "it isn't as if you could hide four hundred banknotes in a . . . unless . . ."

"Unless he separated them. One here, one there," said Dr. Ben helpfully. "Four hundred different hiding places."

Eve shook her head. "No, Ben. From hints he dropped to me, I'm sure he put them in one place, in a roll."

"Hints," said Ellery. "Hints, Miss Warren?"

"Oh, I don't know—cryptic remarks. About clues and things—"

"Clues!"

"Clues," gasped Eve guiltily. "Oh, dear!"

"He left a *clue?*"

"Think, Eve!" implored Dr. Ben.

"It was right in this room. I was reading to him—"

"Reading what?" Ellery asked sharply.

"Something by Poe. . . . Oh, yes, *The Purloined Letter*. And Uncle Malachi laughed, and he said—"

"His exact words, if you can recall them!"

"He said, 'Clever rascal, that Dupin. The most obvious place, eh? Very good! Fact is, there's a clue to my hiding place, Evie, and it's in this very room—the clue, I mean, *not* the money.' And he held his sides laughing. 'In the most obvious place imaginable!' He laughed so hard I thought he'd have a heart attack."

"Clue in the most obvious place in this room . . . Books. He must have meant in one of these thousands of books. But which one!" Ellery stared at Eve. Then he sprang from the chair. "Puns and tricks, you'd said. Of course. . . ." And he began hunting wildly among the mountains and valleys of books, toppling volumes like a landslide. "But he's *got* to be here. . . . Why, Doctor. You're sitting on him!"

Dr. Ben leaped from the Uniform Edition on which he had been seated as if it had suddenly wiggled.

Ellery dropped to his knees, shuffling through the various books of the set. "Ah!" And he sat down on the floor with one of the volumes, clutching it like a roc's egg. First he explored the binding with the tip of his nose. Then he went through the book page by page. Finally he turned back to one of the front pages and read it to himself, mumbling.

When he looked up, Eve and Dr. Ben cried in one voice, "Well?"

"I'm going to ask some questions. Kindly refrain from

hilarity and answer as if your future depended on it—which it does." Ellery consulted the page. "Is there a potted palm any-where in or about the premises?"

"Potted palm?" said Dr. Ben feebly.

"No," said Eve, glaring at her beloved.

"No potted palm. How about a room with a skylight?"

"Skylight . . ."

"No."

"In that art stuff downstairs—ceramics, statuettes, vases—do you recall any object in the shape, or illustrated with the picture of, a dog? A yellow dog?"

"Now there's a blue horse," began Dr. Ben, "with a chipped—"

"No, Mr. Queen!"

"Bows and arrows? Archery target? Picture or statue of an archer? Or a statue of Cupid? Or a door painted green?"

"*Ben.* Not one of those things, Mr. Queen!"

"Clocks," murmured Ellery, glancing again at the book.

"Say," said Dr. Ben. "Dozens of 'em!"

"And I've examined them all," said Ellery, "and none of them conceals the hoard. That being the case," Ellery got to his feet, smiling, "and Uncle Malachi having been fond of his little joke, only one possibility remains."

"What?" asked Uncle Malachi's heirs in a united voice.

"Swiping a leaf from Malachi's rule-of-the-obvious," con-tinued Ellery, "in which of these thousands of books could his clue be hidden? Well, what was the nature of his treasure? Four million dollars. Four million—book. And among these standard sets is the complete works of O. Henry. And one of O. Henry's most famous books is entitled . . . *The Four Mil-lion.*" Ellery waved the volume. "I found nothing foreign in the book. Then the clue was in its contents. Obvious development: see Contents Page. And the titles of the various stories? *Tobin's Palm*—so I asked about a potted palm. *The Skylight Room*—but no skylight. *Memoirs of a Yellow Dog*—no yellow dog. *Mammon and the Archer—The Green Door—The Caliph, Cupid and the Clock*: all fizzled. Only one other possibility among the stories, so that must be Malachi's clue to the hiding place of the cash. *Between Rounds.*"

"*Between Rounds,*" said Dr. Ben, biting his nails. "How the deuce does that tell you anything? Malachi wasn't a prize-fighter, or a—"

"But he was," said Ellery, smiling, "a punster and high priest of the obscurely obvious. Rounds . . . A round is anything that's circular or spherical in shape. What in a pawnshop—in any and every pawnshop—is spherical and large enough to conceal four hundred banknotes?" Eve gasped and ran to the front window. From its rusty arm, which pointed accusingly at the Third Avenue El, hung the ancient emblem of Uncle Malachi's profession. "If you'll find me some tools, Doctor, we'll open those three gilt balls!"

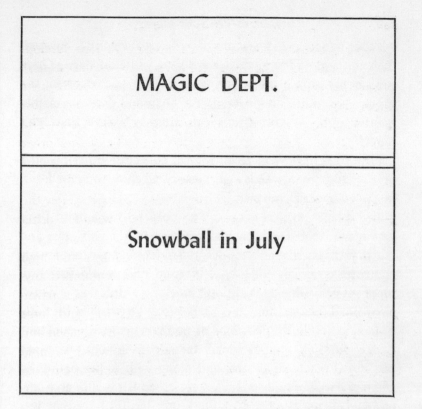

MAGIC DEPT.

Snowball in July

A T PLAYFUL MOMENTS Diamond Jim Grady liked to refer to himself as a magician, a claim no one disputed—least of all the police. Grady's specialty was jewel robbery at gunpoint, a branch of felonious vaudeville which he had elevated to an art form. His heists were miracles of advance information, timing, teamwork, and deception. And once he got his hands on the loot it vanished with the speed of light, to be seen no more in the shape the manufacturing jeweler had wrought.

Grady's most spectacular trick was keeping himself and his fellow artists out of jail. He would drill his small company without mercy in the wisdom of keeping their mugs covered, their mitts gloved, and their traps shut while on stage. There was rarely a slip in his performances; when one occurred, the slipping assistant disappeared. As Diamond Jim reasonably pointed out, "What witness 'can identify a slob that ain't here?"

Grady might have gone on forever collecting other people's pretties and driving the law and insurance companies mad, but he pulled one trick too many.

In explanation it is necessary to peep into Diamond Jim's love life. Lizbet had been his big moment for two years and ten months—a slim eyestopper as golden and glittery as any choice piece in his collection. Now in underworld society a romantic attachment of almost three years' duration is equivalent to an epic passion, and Lizbet may be forgiven the folly of having developed delusions of permanence. Unfortunately, that was not all she developed; include an appetite for pizza pies and French ice cream, and along with it her figure. So when one night Grady's bloated eye cased the dainty anatomy of Maybellene, pivot girl of the Club Swahili line, that was all for Lizbet.

One of Grady's staff, a lovelorn lapidary who could grind an ax as well as a diamond, tipped Lizbet the bad news from a phone booth in the Swahili men's room even as Diamond Jim prepared toothily to escort Maybellene home.

Lizbet was revolted at the perfidy of man. She also realized that unless she lammed with great rapidity her life was not worth the crummiest bangle on the junk counter of the nearest Five-and-Dime. She knew far, far too many of Diamond Jim's professional secrets; she even knew where a couple of bodies— of ex-slobs—were buried.

So Lizbet took barely the time to grab an old summer mink and a fistful of unaltered mementoes from Grady's latest personal appearance before she did an impromptu vanishing act of her own.

Immediately Lizbet became the most popular girl in town. Everybody wanted her, especially the police and Grady. The smart money, doping past performances strictly, was on Grady, but this time the smart money took a pratfall. Lizbet was not in town at all. She was in Canada, where—according to every Royal Northwest movie Lizbet had ever seen—the Mounties were large and incorruptible and a girl could think without worrying about stopping a shiv with her back. Having thought, Lizbet slung the summer mink about her plump shoulders, taxied to the nearest police station, and demanded protection and immunity in exchange for a pledge to take the witness stand back home and talk herself, if need be, into lockjaw.

And she insisted on being ushered into a cell while Montreal got in touch with New York.

The long distance negotiations took twenty-four hours. Just long enough for the news to leak out and inundate the front pages of the New York newspapers.

"So now Grady knows where she is," fumed Inspector Queen. He was on special assignment in charge of the case. "He'll go for her sure. She told Piggott and Hesse when they flew up to Montreal that she can even drape a first-degree murder rap around Grady's fat neck."

"Me," said Sergeant Velie gloomily, "I wouldn't give a plugged horse car token for that broad's chances of getting back to New York with a whole hide."

"What is he, a jet pilot?" asked Ellery. "Fly her down."

"She won't fly, has a fear of heights," snapped his father. "It's on the level, Ellery. Lizbet's the only girl friend Grady ever had who turned down a penthouse."

"Train or car, then," said Ellery. "What's the hassle?"

"A train he'd make hash out of," said Sergeant Velie, "and a car he'd hijack some truck to run off the road into a nice thousand-foot hole."

"You're romancing."

"Maestro, you don't know Grady!"

"Then you're tackling this hind end to," said Ellery negligently. "Dad, have Grady and his gang picked up on some charge and locked in a cell. By the time they're sprung this woman can be safe on ice somewhere in Manhattan."

"On ice is where she'll wind up," said Sergeant Velie. "And speaking of ice, who's for a bucket of Thomas Collins?"

When Ellery found that Diamond Jim had anticipated interference and disappeared with his entire company, including Maybellene, a respectful glint came into his eye.

"Let's pull a trick or two of our own. Grady will assume that you'll get Lizbet to New York as quickly as possible. He knows she won't fly and that you wouldn't risk the long trip by car. So he'll figure she'll be brought down by rail. Since the fastest way by rail is a through express, it's the crack Montreal train he'll be gunning for. Does he know Piggott and Hesse by sight?"

"Let's say he does," said Inspector Queen, perking up notwithstanding the heat, "and I see what you mean. I'll fly Johnson and Goldberg up there along with a policewoman of Lizbet's build and general appearance. Piggott and Hesse take the policewoman onto the Special, heavily veiled, while Goldie and Johnson hustle Lizbet onto a slow train—"

"You think this Houdini plays with potsies?" demanded Sergeant Velie. "You got to do better than that, my masters."

"Oh, come, Sergeant, he's only flesh and blood," said Ellery soothingly. "Anyway, we're going to do better than that. To befuddle him completely, somewhere along the route we'll have her taken off and complete the trip by automobile. In fact, Dad, we'll take her off ourselves. Feel better, Velie?"

But the Sergeant shook his head. "You don't know Grady."

So Detectives Goldberg and Johnson and an ex-chorus girl named Policewoman Bruusgaard flew to Montreal, and at the zero hour Detectives Piggott and Hesse ostentatiously spirited Policewoman Bruusgaard—veiled and sweltering in Lizbet's mink—into a drawing room on the Canadian Limited. Thirty minutes after the Limited rolled out of the terminal Detectives Johnson and Goldberg, attired as North Country backwoodsmen and lugging battered suitcases, swaggered behind Lizbet into the smoking car of a sooty, suffocating all-coach local-express entitled laughingly in the timetables The Snowball. Lizbet was in dowdy clothes, her coiffure was now blue-black, and her streaming face—scrubbed clean of heavy makeup—seemed a sucker's bet to fool even Grady, so many wrinkles and crow's-feet showed.

And the game was en route.

For on a sizzling hot morning in July two unmarked squad cars set out from Center Street, Manhattan, for upstate New York. In one rode the Queens and Sergeant Velie, in the other six large detectives.

The Sergeant drove lugubriously. "It won't work," he predicted. "He operates practically by radar. And he can spot and grease an itchy palm from nine miles up. I tell you Grady's got this up his sleeve right now."

"You croak like a witch doctor with bellyache," remarked Inspector Queen, squirming in his damp clothes. "Just remember, Velie, if we don't get to Wapaug with time to spare—"

Wapaug was a whistlestop on the C. & N. Y. Railroad. It consisted of several simmering coal piles, a straggly single street, and a roasted-looking cubby of a station. The two cars drove up to the brown little building and the Inspector and Ellery went inside. No one was in the hotbox of a waiting room but an elderly man wearing sleeve garters and an eyeshade who was poking viciously at the innards of a paralyzed electric fan.

"What's with The Snowball?"

"Number 113? On time, mister."

"And she's due—?"

"10:18."

"Three minutes," said Ellery. "Let's go."

The cars had drawn up close, one to each end of the platform. Two of the six detectives were leaning exhaustedly against an empty handtruck. Otherwise, the baked platform was deserted.

They all squinted north.

10:18 came.

10:18 went.

At 10:20 they were still squinting north.

The stationmaster was in the doorway now, also squinting north.

"Hey!" rasped Inspector Queen, swatting a mosquito. "Where was that train on time? In Vermont?"

"At Grove Junction." The stationmaster peered up the tracks, which looked as if they had just come out of a blast furnace. "Where the yards and roundhouse are. It's the all-train stop two stations north."

"Train 113 stops at the next station north, too, doesn't she? Marmion? Did you get a report on her from Marmion?"

"I was just gonna check, mister."

They followed him back into the hotbox and the elderly man put on his slippery headphones and got busy with the telegraph key. "Marmion stationmaster says she pulled in and out on time. Left Marmion 10:12."

"On time at Marmion," said Ellery, "and it's only a six-minute run from Marmion to Wapaug—" He wiped his neck.

"Funny," fretted his father. It was now 10:22. "How could she lose four minutes on a six-minute run? Even on this railroad?"

"Somethin's wrong," said the stationmaster, blowing the sweat off his eyeshade band. He turned suddenly to his key.

The Queens returned to the platform to stare up the local track toward Marmion. After a moment Ellery hurried back into the waiting room.

"Stationmaster, could she have switched to the express track at Marmion and gone right through Wapaug without stopping?" He knew the answer in advance, since they had driven along the railroad for miles in their approach to Wapaug; but his brains were frying.

"Nothin's gone through southbound on these tracks since 7:38 this mornin'."

Ellery hurried out again, fingering his collar. His father was sprinting up the platform toward the squad car. The two detectives had already rejoined their mates in the other car and it was roaring up the highway, headed north.

"Come on!" shouted Inspector Queen. Ellery barely made it

before Sergeant Velie sent the car rocketing toward the road. "Somehow Grady got onto the trick—a smear, a leak at headquarters! He's waylaid The Snowball between here and Marmion—wrecked it!"

They kept watching the ties. The automobile road paralleled the railroad at a distance of barely twenty feet, with nothing between but gravel.

And there was no sign of a passenger train, in motion or standing still, wrecked or whole. Or of a freight, or even a handcar. Headed south—or, for that matter, headed north.

They almost zoomed through Marmion before they realized that they had covered the entire distance between the two stations. The other car was parked below the weathered eaves of an even smaller shed than the one at Wapaug. As they shot back in reverse, four of the detectives burst out of the little station.

"She left Marmion at 10:12, all right, Inspector!" yelled one. "Stationmaster says we're crazy. We must have missed it!"

The two cars rocked about and raced back toward Wapaug.

Inspector Queen glared at the rails flashing alongside. "Missed it? A whole passenger train? Velie, slow down—!"

"That Grady," moaned Sergeant Velie.

Ellery devoured a knuckle and said nothing. He kept staring at the glittering rails. They winked back, jeering. It was remarkable how straight this stretch of track between Marmion and Wapaug was, how uncluttered by scenery. Not a tree or building beside the right of way. No water anywhere, not so much as a rain puddle. No curves, no grades; no siding, spur line, tunnel, bridge. Not a gully, gorge, or ravine. And no sign of wreckage . . . The rails stretched, perfect and unburdened, along the hellish floor of the valley. For all the concealment or trickery possible, they might have been a series of parallel lines drawn with a ruler on a sheet of blank paper.

And there was Wapaug's roasted little station again.

And no Snowball.

The Inspector's voice cracked. "She pulls into Grove Junction on time. She gets to Marmion on time. She pulls out of Marmion on time. But she doesn't show up at Wapaug. Then she's got to be between Marmion and Wapaug! What's wrong with that?" He challenged them, hopefully, to find something wrong with it.

Sergeant Velie accepted. "Only one thing," he said in a hollow voice. "She ain't."

That did it. "I suppose Grady's palmed it!" screamed his superior. "That train's between Marmion and Wapaug somewhere, and I'm going to find it or—or buy me a ouija board!"

So back they went to Marmion, driving along the railroad at ten miles per hour. And then they turned around and crept Wapaugward again, to shuffle into the waiting room and look piteously at the stationmaster. But that railroad man was sitting in his private oven mopping his chafed forehead and blinking at the shimmering valley through his north window.

And no one said a word for some time.

When the word came, everyone leaped. "Stationmaster!" said Ellery. "Get your Marmion man on that key again. Find out if, after leaving Marmion at 10:12, *The Snowball didn't turn back.*"

"Back?" The elderly man brightened. "Sure!" He seized his telegraph key.

"That's it, Ellery!" cried Inspector Queen. "She left Marmion southbound all right, but then she backed up north *past*

Marmion again for a repair, and I'll bet she's in the Grove Junction yards or roundhouse right now!"

"Grove Junction says," whispered the stationmaster, "that she ain't in their yards or roundhouse and never was—just went through on time. And Marmion says 113 pulled out southbound and she didn't come back."

And all were silent once more.

But then the Inspector slapped at a dive-bombing squadron of bluebottle flies, hopping on one foot and howling. "But how can a whole train disappear? Snowball! Snowball in July! What did Grady do, melt her down for ice water?"

"And drank her," said Sergeant Velie, licking his lips.

"Wait," said Ellery. "Wait . . . I know where The Snowball is!" He scuttled toward the door. "And if I'm right we'd better make tracks—or kiss Lizbet goodbye!"

"But *where?*" implored Inspector Queen as the two cars flashed north again, toward Marmion.

"Down Grady's gullet," shouted the Sergeant, wrestling his wheel.

"That's what he wanted us to think," shouted Ellery in reply. "Faster, Sergeant! Train leaves Marmion and never shows up at the next station south, where we're waiting to take Lizbet off. Vanishes without a trace. Between Marmion and Wapaug there's nothing at all to explain what could have happened to her—no bridge to fall from, no water or ravine to fall into, no tunnel to hide in, no anything—just a straight line on flat bare country. Marvelous illusion. Only the same facts that give it the appearance of magic explain it. . . . No, Velie, don't slow down," Ellery yelled as the dreary little Marmion station came into view. "Keep going north—*past* Marmion!"

"North past Marmion?" said his father, bewildered. "But the train came *through* Marmion, Ellery, headed south . . ."

"The Snowball's nowhere south of Marmion, is it? And from the facts it's a physical impossibility for her to be anywhere south of Marmion. So she *isn't* south of Marmion, Dad. *She never went through Marmion at all.*"

"But the Marmion stationmaster said—"

"What Grady bribed him to say! It was all a trick to keep us running around in circles between Marmion and Wapaug, while Grady and his gang held up the train *between Marmion and Grove Junction!* Isn't that gunfire up ahead? We're still in time!"

And there, four miles north of Marmion, where the valley entered the foothills, cowered The Snowball, frozen to the spot. A huge trailer-truck dumped athwart the local tracks had stopped her, and judging from the gun flashes she was under bombardment of half a dozen bandits hidden in the woods nearby.

Two figures, one lying still and the other crawling toward the woods dragging a leg, told them that the battle was not one-sided. From two of the shattered windows of a railroad car a stream of bullets poured into the woods. What Grady & Co. had not known was that Northwoodsmen Goldberg and Johnson had carried in their battered suitcases two submachine guns and a large supply of ammunition.

When the carful of New York detectives broke out their arsenal and cut loose on the run, the Grady gang dropped their weapons and trudged out with their dejected arms up. . . .

Ellery and the Inspector found Lizbet huddled on the floor of the smoking car with assorted recumbent passengers, in a litter of hot cartridge shells, while Detectives Johnson and Goldberg prepared rather shakily to enjoy a couple of stained cigarets.

"You all right, young woman?" asked the Inspector anxiously. "Anything I can get you?"

Lizbet looked up out of a mess of dyed hair, gunsmoke, sweat, and tears. "You said it, pop," she hissed. "That witness chair!"

FALSE CLAIMANT DEPT.

The Witch of Times Square

I‍F LAST YEAR you had asked Father Bowen of All Souls-off-Times Square whether or not he subscribed to the Deuteronomic doctrine of an eye for an eye, he would have rebuked you—being a good Anglican—and cited some King Jamesian reminder, probably *Matthew, v, 38–39*, on the Case of the Reversible Cheek. Put the question to him today and Father Bowen is more likely to rub a leathery grin into his jaw and quote that profane authority, Ellery Queen, on the Case of the False Claimant.

Father Bowen's flock being pastured in the West Forties, it is plentifully mixed with black sheep. Until last year one of his sorriest blessings was a gay old ewe known to the touts, newspaper vendors, bartenders, carny boys, cops, and other habitués of Broadway as the Witch—a hag with lank gray-blonde locks, cheeks like bark, and runny blue eyes, who wore sidewalk-length skirts, an outrageous shawl, and a man's fedora which came from some night club trash can. The Witch lived alone in a basement hole over toward Tenth Avenue, and she bounded forth at night to sell violets, corsages of gardenias, and policy tickets under the marquees and neon signs. Toward morning—she was of English blood, her name being Wichingame—she could usually be found at some all-night bar before a long row of empty gin-and-tonic glasses, singing "Brightest and Best of the Sons of the Morning" or "The Church's One Foundation" in a hoarse, joyful voice. Her record of attendance at All Souls-off-Times Square was not meritorious, although she could always be depended upon in the confessional, where she went into enthusiastic clinical detail.

Her pastor labored hard in this exasperating vineyard, but he had no cause to rejoice until one winter week, when the Witch mistook the new snowfall on her sidewalk for the coverlet of her bed and awakened in Bellevue Hospital with a case of double lobar pneumonia. She was very ill, and at some time during her sojourn in the Valley she saw the Light. She sent for Father Bowen, who hastened to cultivate this most stubborn of his vines; and when she clanged home in a jubilant ambulance, Father Bowen holding her hand, she was a permanently repentant sinner.

"Then what's the problem, Father Bowen?" asked Ellery, wincing as he tried to turn over in bed. He had been laid up for ten days by a painful attack of sciatica, and he had been about to go mad when the clergyman called.

"The root of the problem, Mr. Queen," said Father Bowen, hooking his bony arm under Ellery's and lifting expertly, "is the love of money. See *I Timothy, vi,* 10. It turns out that Miss Wichingame is—as they say in my parish—loaded. She owns several immensely valuable parcels of property and a considerable amount of cash and bonds. The poor thing has been, of course, a miser. Now, in her spiritual regeneration, she insists on giving it all away."

"To some needy bartender, Father?"

"I almost wish that were it," said the old clergyman with a sigh. "I know at least three whose needs are great. But no—it's to go to her only living heir." And Father Bowen told Ellery the curious story of the Witch's nephew.

Miss Wichingame had had a twin sister, and while they were identical in every physical respect, their tastes differed profoundly. Miss Wichingame, for example, had early shown a preference for gin and the wilder variety of oat, whereas her twin looked upon spirits as the devil's lubricant and was as moral as a breakfast cereal.

This disparity, unfortunately for Miss Wichingame, extended to their tastes in men. Miss Wichingame fell in love with a small, handsome, dark man—an Italian, or Spaniard; after forty-five years she could not recall which—but her sister, whose firm eugenic credo was "like to like," gave her maiden heart to "a pure Nordic," as Miss Wichingame told Father Bowen—one Erik Gaard, of Fergus Falls, Minnesota, a large sedate Viking who had gone over to the Anglican church and become a missionary priest. Miss Wichingame's Italian, or Spaniard, turned out a scoundrel who left her unwed and with pleasant if not entirely respectable memories; the Reverend Gaard, no trifler, proposed holy matrimony to Miss Wichingame's sister and was triumphantly accepted.

A son was born to the Gaards, and when he was eight years old his parents sailed him to the Orient. For a short time the missionary's wife corresponded with her twin, but as Miss Wichingame's address became increasingly fluid the letters from the mission in Korea took longer and longer to catch up with her, until finally they stopped altogether.

"I take it," said Ellery, cautiously shifting his left leg, "that when your communicant repented her sins she asked you to locate her sister."

"I instituted inquiries through our missionary branch," said Father Bowen, nodding, "and discovered that Father Gaard and his wife were murdered many years ago—the pre-war Japanese made it very difficult for Christian missionaries in Korea—and that their mission was burned to the ground. Their son, John, was believed to have escaped to China, although no trace of him was found.

"My parishioner," continued Father Bowen, and he became agitated, "revealed at this point an unexpected firmness of character. She insisted that her nephew was alive and that he must be found and brought to the United States, so that she might embrace him before she died and give him all her money. Perhaps you recall the newspaper publicity, Mr. Queen, especially among the columnists. I shall not try your patience with the details of our search—it was expensive and hopeless . . . hopeless, that is, to one of little faith, like myself; for Miss Wichingame's part, I must say she was perfectly confident through it all."

"And Nephew John was found."

"Yes, Mr. Queen. Two of him."

"I beg your pardon?"

"He appeared at my rectory in two installments, as it were, each part of him fresh from Korea, and each part of him insisting *he* was John Gaard, son of Erik and Clementine Gaard, and that the other fellow was a cheeky impostor. An embarrassment of blessings. Frankly, I'm up the creek."

"I suppose they look alike?"

"Not the least bit. While both are blond and about thirty-five—the correct age—there's no resemblance at all, either to each other or to Father and Mrs. Gaard, an old photo of whom exists. But there is no authenticated photograph of John Gaard, so even their dissimilarity doesn't help."

"But I should think," protested Ellery, "visas, passports, ordinary proofs of identity, records of background—"

"You forget, Mr. Queen," said Father Bowen with a certain steeliness, "that Korea in recent years has not been exactly a garden of tranquillity. The two young men, it appears, had been close friends, both having worked for the same oil company in China. When the Chinese Communists closed in, they fled—quite irregularly—to Korea. The North Korean invasion caught them there, and they got out with a mob of refugees after the Communist armies first took Seoul. There was a great deal of official confusion and a relaxation of the normal precautions. Each young man exhibits documents in the name of John Gaard, and each came out by plane through a different airfield."

"How do they explain the identical documents?"

"Each says the other stole his credentials and had them duplicated—except, of course, for the passport photographs. Each says he told the other of an aunt in the United States.

No checkup can be made in Korea and, unfortunately, the oil company records in China are not accessible. All our inquiries of the Chinese Communist authorities, made through diplomatic intermediaries, have been ignored. You may take my word for it, Mr. Queen, there's simply no way of checking back on their identities."

Ellery was surprised to find himself sitting up in bed, a position he had been unable to achieve in over a week. "And the Witch?" he exclaimed.

"Bewildered, Mr. Queen. The last time she saw her nephew was when he was seven years old, just before his parents took him to the Far East. He spent an exciting week in New York with her—during which week, by the way, she kept a diary. She still has it—"

"There you are," said Ellery. "All she has to do is question each man about that week. The genuine one surely remembers something of such a great boyhood adventure."

"She has done so," said Father Bowen sorrowfully. "Each recalls part of it. Each claims with dismaying bitterness that the other can answer such questions because he told him all about it—forgive me if my pronouns are confused. The poor woman has quite worn herself out trying to trip one of them up. She's ready to divide her money between them—and I won't have that!" said the old shepherd sternly. "Can you see a way out, Mr. Queen?"

Ellery asked every question he could think of, and he thought of a great many.

"Well, Father," he said at last, shaking his head, and Father Bowen's lean face fell, "I don't see . . ." And suddenly he stopped shaking his head.

"Yes?" cried the clergyman.

"Or maybe I do! A way to get at the truth . . . yes . . . Where are the two Johns now, Father?"

"At my rectory."

"Could you have them here in, say, an hour?"

"Oh, yes," said Father Bowen grimly. "Oh, yes, indeed!"

One hour later the aged cleric herded two angry-looking young men into Ellery's bedroom and shut the door with a sinister little snick.

"I've had a lot of trouble keeping them from manhandling each other, Mr. Queen. This, gentlemen, is Ellery Queen," said Father Bowen coldly, "and *he'll* soon put an end to this nonsense!"

"I don't care who he is and what he says," growled the first young man. "I'm John Gaard."

"You dug-up *shi*," bellowed the second young man, "you took those words right out of my mouth!"

"Did you ever get your head knocked off by a corpse?"

"Try it, you—"

"Would you two stand side by side, please," said Ellery, "facing that window?"

They grew quiet.

Ellery looked them over sharply. The first young man was blond and tall, with big shoulders, sun-squinted brown eyes, a snub nose, and huge feet and work-battered hands. The second was short and sandy-haired, squintily blue-eyed and curve-nosed, with small feet and clever-looking hands. They were as unlike as two kittens in an alley litter, but two pairs of fists were at the ready, and both glowered, and it was impossible to say which seemed more honestly outraged, the Witch's nephew or his impostor.

"You see?" said Father Bowen despairingly.

"Indeed I do, Father," said Ellery, smiling through his travail, "and I'll be happy to identify John Gaard for you."

The young men glared, as if daring each other to make a break for it.

"It's all right, gentlemen," said Ellery, "there's a very large detective-sergeant named Tom Velie waiting in the next room who could break the back of either of you without dropping the ash from his cigaret. How do I know, did you ask, Father Bowen?"

"Why, yes, Mr. Queen," said the clergyman, bewildered. "You haven't asked these young men a single question."

"Would you mind reaching to that shelf, Father," said Ellery with another smile, "and handing me that great, fat, ominous-looking book in the plain paper wrapper? . . . Thank you. . . . This volume, gentlemen, is forbiddingly entitled *Forensic Medicine and Legal Biology*, and it was written by two of the foremost authorities in the field, Mendelius and Claggett. Let's see, it should be around page five hundred and something. . . . Why, Father, you told me that Miss Wichingame's twin sister was identical with her in every physical respect. Since Miss Wichingame is blue-eyed, then Mrs. Gaard must have been blue-eyed, too. And you described the Reverend Gaard in Miss Wichingame's words as 'a pure Nordic,' which ethnologically puts John Gaard's father among the blue-eyed, too. . . . Ah, here it is. Now let me read you the second paragraph on page five sixty-three of this authoritative work.

"*Two blue-eyed persons*," Ellery said, his eyes on the open page of the big book, "*would produce only children with blue eyes. They would not produce children with brown eyes.*"

"There he goes!" cried Father Bowen.

"Velie!" roared Ellery. "Catch him!"

And Sergeant Velie, appearing magically, did so in his usual emphatic manner.

While the Sergeant was leading the tall, broad, brown-eyed impostor away, and the short, blue-eyed, authenticated John Gaard was trying to express his thanks to Ellery in an excited mixture of English, Chinese, and Korean, Father Bowen picked up the fat book from Ellery's bed, which Ellery had closed, and he turned to page 563. A look of perplexity wrinkled his leathery face, and he removed the paper jacket and glanced at the cover.

"But Mr. Queen," exclaimed Father Bowen, "this book isn't entitled *Forensic Medicine and Legal Biology*. It's an old edition of *Who's Who!*"

"Is it?" said Ellery guiltily. "I could have sworn—"

"Don't," said Father Bowen in a severe tone. "The fact is Mendelius and Claggett don't exist. You just made that whole quotation about blue eyes-brown eyes up! Isn't it true?"

"There was a time when the books said it was," said Ellery mournfully, "but they probably don't any more—too many blue-eyed parents of irreproachable probity were turning up with brown-eyed children. However, our brown-eyed claimant didn't know that, Father, did he? And now," Ellery said to blue-eyed young John, who was gaping idiotically, "I'll name my fee: Turn me over in this damned—beg pardon, Father— bed!"

RACKET DEPT.

The Gamblers' Club

THE LIFE of The Gamblers' Club was a merry one. It was correspondingly short, and when overnight the Club ceased to exist speculation ran up and down the gamut searching for an explanation. But the ex-membership had taken a terrible oath, more binding than if it had been sworn in blood, and no traitor to the conspiracy of silence could be found. For these were businessmen, and they could hardly confess that in the clutch their roster—most of whom were self-made millionaires only lately retired from their exertions—had failed in simple arithmetic.

Ellery was admitted into the sacred mysteries of The Gamblers' Club one winter morning, when a stainless town car which the slush of 87th Street seemed unable to sully deposited three men on his doorstep. Inspector Queen, who was home that morning working on a confidential report to the Commissioner, raised his birdy brows at the size of the car and retired with his papers to the study—not, however, without leaving the door ajar the irreducible minimum for eavesdropping.

The three men introduced themselves as Charles Van Wyne, Cornelius Lewis, and Gorman Fitch. Van Wyne was slender and bluish, Lewis was huge and brown, and Fitch was roly-poly and pink. Where Van Wyne had a crumbly look, like a rare cheese prominently displayed in a Park Avenue gourmet's shop, Lewis was a rich brute roast served on a Wall Street table; and as for Fitch, with his puffy pinkness he looked uncannily like Ellery's recollection of the boyhood confection known as Foxy Grandpa—Fitch had made his money, he announced immediately, in brassières.

The Gamblers' Club, they explained to Ellery, was an association of seventeen retired men with a passion for gambling and the means to indulge it. In addition to the conventional group games of chance played in the clubrooms, members were pledged to suggest unusual gambling adventures to one another on an individual basis, being expected in this oath-bound obligation to display imagination and ingenuity. Suggestions were made by mail, anonymously, on special letterheads of The Gamblers' Club available to members only.

"Why anonymously?" asked Ellery, fascinated.

"Well, when someone's been hurt," squeaked pink little Mr.

Fitch, "we don't want him holding a grudge against the suggesting member."

"Of course, we're all reliable characters," murmured Van Wyne, nibbling the head of his stick. "Wouldn't be possible otherwise, you know. Quite the point of the Club."

"Apparently someone's developed an unreliable streak," observed Ellery, "or you gentlemen wouldn't be here."

The trio exchanged glances.

"You tell it, Van Wyne," boomed the large Mr. Lewis.

"Lewis dropped in on me this morning," said Van Wyne abruptly, "to ask if I happened to be party to a certain individual Club gamble he'd been enjoying, and when we compared notes we found we were both in the same thing. The two of us wondered if anyone else was in it, and since Mr. Fitch lives in my neighborhood we dropped in on him and, sure enough, he was involved, too.

"Exactly three weeks ago each of us received a long envelope in the morning mail, with a typewritten message on Club stationery—quite in order—giving us a tip on the market. The stock suggested is unstable as the deuce, way up one day and way down the next, making it a real gamble, so each of us bought. It took a big jump, and we cleaned up.

"Two weeks ago this morning we each received a second letter proposing the purchase of another stock, equally jittery. Two days later this stock zoomed, and again we made a lot of money.

"And just one week ago today—"

"The same thing," rumbled Cornelius Lewis impatiently.

"You want to know," asked Ellery, "how he does it?"

"Oh, we know how he does it," said pudgy Mr. Fitch testily. "He's got inside information, of course. It's not that—"

"Then it's the letter you all received this morning."

The big ex-banker glowered. "How the devil did you know we got letters from him today, too?"

"Let's call him Mr. X," said Ellery, getting into the spirit of the thing. "Mr. X's first letter came three weeks ago today, his second two weeks ago today, his third one week ago today—so it was a pretty good bet, Mr. Lewis, that a fourth came today. What's disturbing you about it, gentlemen?"

Charles Van Wyne produced a long envelope.

"Read it, Mr. Queen, and settle an argument."

The envelope was of fine quality. It had no imprint or return address. Van Wyne's name and address were typewritten, and from the postmark it had been mailed the previous night.

Ellery removed from it a sheet of weighty stationery with a tony *The Gamblers' Club* at the top in gold engraving:

Dear Fellow Member:

How did you like my three market tips? Now something new has come up and it looks like the best yet. Secrecy is important, though, and I have to handle it personally or it's all off. If you'll gamble $25,000 on a hot chance to double it in seven days, no questions asked, wrap the cash in a waterproof package and leave it at the foot of Dominicus Pike's grave in Trinity churchyard tomorrow at 3:30 a.m. on the button. No prying, or you'll spoil the deal.

There was no signature.

"Now I've told Lewis," said Van Wyne, "that this is a sporting gamble. The man's proved himself. I'm for it."

"I don't say I'm not," growled Cornelius Lewis. "The only thing is—"

"Isn't that why we're here?" demanded Gorman Fitch with a sniff. "What do you think, Queen? This sound on the level to you?"

"Fitch, you're impugning the integrity of a fellow member," said Van Wyne coldly.

"I'm just asking a question!"

"It's possible, Van Wyne, isn't it?" grumbled Lewis. "And if somebody's turned crooked, that's the end of the Club and you know it. What's your opinion, Queen?"

"Sounds awfully good to me," murmured Ellery. "But I'd want to dig a bit before committing myself. Did either of you other gentlemen bring your letters of this morning with you?"

"Left mine home," stated Lewis.

"They're practically identical with Van Wyne's," objected Fitch.

"I'd like to see them, nevertheless, envelope and all. Suppose you send them right over to me by messenger. I'll phone the three of you before noon."

The moment the front door had closed, the study door opened; and there was Inspector Queen, incredulous.

"Did I hear right?" snapped Ellery's father. "Did you say to those three this sounds 'awfully good' to you? Good for what, laughs?"

"The trouble with you," said Ellery in a pained way, "is that you've got no gambling blood. Why not wait for developments?"

Emerging from the study again just before noon, Inspector Queen found his celebrated son examining two envelopes and their contents. Cornelius Lewis's envelope, postmarked the night before, was exactly like the one Charles Van Wyne had received, and the wording on the Club letterhead was the same except that where Van Wyne's time for depositing the $25,000 at the Trinity Church grave had been 3:30 A.M., Lewis's was to be 3:45 A.M. The small plain envelope Gorman Fitch had received, also postmarked the previous night, contained the same message on Club stationery except that Fitch was to deposit his package of cash at 4:00 A.M.

"I suppose," said the Inspector, "you're going to recommend that your three potsy-playing clients follow these awfully good instructions to the letter?"

"Sure thing," said Ellery cheerfully; and to the Inspector's stupefaction Ellery telephoned to Van Wyne, Lewis, and Fitch in turn, informing each that in his professional opinion the gamble was as safe as Fort Knox and he only wished he had the entree—and the $25,000—to gamble with them.

"Are you out of your mind, Ellery?" howled Inspector Queen as Ellery hung up for the third time. "The only sure thing in this racket is that three suckers are going to be taken for twenty-five thousand lollypops apiece!"

"Racket?" murmured the son.

The old gentleman controlled himself. "Look. This smoothie operates on a group of fish—"

"Mr. X? And what do you mean by 'group'? Specify."

"Seventeen! One of the seventeen Club members has gone sour. Maybe he's broke. He works out a con scheme, the basis of which is market tips to the other sixteen members. He picks a stock that's always acting like a pogo stick and he writes half the members to play this stock to go up, the other half to play it to go down. Whichever way the stock moves, up or down, half the members lose, *but the other half win,* and with the winners he's a genius.

"Step two: He ignores the losers in the first operation and sends his second tip, on another ultra-lively stock, only to the winners—"

"Figures," pleaded Ellery. "Exactly how many would receive the second tip?"

"Half the original sixteen! Eight, the eight first winners. Now he tips half these eight to play the stock up, the other half to play it down. Again, half have to win—"

"Number, please," said Ellery.

"Can't you do kindergarten arithmetic? Half of eight is four! Now he's got four two-time winners. He picks another kangaroo stock, sends the third letter, this time telling half the four to play the stock up, the other half to play it down.

"So now he's got his three-times-winning chumps primed, full of confidence in his market know-how, and he's ready to spring the big one. He sends his fourth letter to the two suckers—"

"To the how many suckers?" inquired Ellery.

"To the two remaining winners!"

"Starting with sixteen fish, that's what it should boil down to, all right," mourned Ellery. "The only thing is, it doesn't. *We've got three.*"

Slowly, the Inspector sat down.

"An extra man," said Ellery. "Question: Who is he, and how could he possibly defy the laws of mathematics? Answer: He can't, so he's the con man himself, our friend Mr. X, not one of the fish at all."

"Van Wyne, Lewis, or Fitch. One of them's the bunco . . ."

"I'm afraid so. Whichever one of the three he is, this morning, to his annoyance, he found himself in a consultation with his two victims. The letters setting up the graveyard payoff had been mailed last night and were already delivered, so he couldn't do anything about *them*. He could only pretend he'd been a three-times winner, too! If I recognized the gimmick when they came to consult me, and if I warned his innocents to lay off, Mr. X would simply fail to show up tonight at Trinity. But if I didn't seem suspicious, or a threat to him, he'd go through with his scheme. Does it figure?"

"Like Einstein," chortled the Inspector; and he hurried downtown to police headquarters to make certain arrangements about a churchyard and the grave of one Dominicus Pike.

Ghosts walked about Broadway and Wall Street that night, but by 1:00 A.M. they had subsided behind various illustrious headstones in the churchyard, and the area grew quiet. Ellery insisted that his father share George Washington's old pew in the chapel with him, murmuring something about the long wintry wait and the Father of Truth.

But at 3:15 the Queens were skulking behind one of Mother Trinity's skirts, shivering with the rest of the ghouls.

At 3:30 A.M. on the nose the slender shadow of Charles Van Wyne fell eagerly across the grave of Dominicus Pike. It deposited something on the frozen ground, slithered away, and was lost.

At 3:45 the black hulk of Cornelius Lewis appeared, dropped something, and fell off.

At the last stroke of 4:00 A.M. the dumpy blur that was Gorman Fitch repeated the process, and then he too disappeared.

"Whichever he is, he's taking no chances," chattered Inspector Queen. "If anything went wrong, he'd be one of the suckers depositing his twenty-five grand. Now he'll wait a while. Then he'll sneak back to pick up all three packages. I wonder which one it'll turn out to be."

"Why, Dad," said Ellery in an amazed undertone, "do you mean to say you don't *know?*"

"No, I don't," whispered the Inspector malevolently. "And don't tell me you do!"

Ellery sighed. "X certainly didn't send any letters to himself—he didn't expect to have to enter the problem as a 'victim' at all. When accident forced him into it yesterday morning, he was in a jam. Yes, he could lie to the other two and *say* he had also received the fourth letter, but I asked him to produce it—along with the envelope. To look genuine, the envelope he gave me had to have the same postmark as the other two—the postmark of the night before! But that was impossible—it was now the morning after.

"So X did the best he could. He looked through his legitimate morning mail and found a plain envelope addressed to him, with no return address, which bore the correct postmark of the previous night; and he sent that envelope along to me with the note he had hastily typed as an enclosure. The only trouble was, the envelope was *of a different size* from the ones he'd been sending his victims. He hoped, I suppose, that I wouldn't notice the discrepancy."

"Van Wyne's envelope was long . . ."

"And Lewis's was identical with Van Wyne's. But the third envelope," said Ellery, "was a *small* envelope, and since that was the one sent over to me by . . ."

A shout profaned the churchyard, lights popped, and in their beams a figure was caught squatting over three bundles on the grave like a boy in a melon patch—the pudgy little figure of Gorman Fitch.

DYING MESSAGE DEPT.

GI Story

Eᴌʟᴇʀʏ sᴡᴜɴɢ ᴏғғ ᴛʜᴇ Atlantic State Express in his favorite small town disguised by earlaps, muffler, and skis, resolved that this time nothing should thwart his winter holiday. But he had hardly dumped his gear in Bill York's Bald Mountain lodge when he was called to the phone. Sure enough, it was Wrightsville's chief of police, with a crime.

"I haven't even taken my hat off," Ellery complained. "What do your criminals do, Dakin, watch the Arrivals column in the *Record?*"

"This one's real unorthodox," said Chief Dakin, in the tone

of one emotionally involved. "Can I send a car right up?"

The lean old Yank was waiting fretfully on State Street at the side entrance to the County Court House. He pulled himself into the police car with one hand and groped for Ellery with the other.

"I've been up most of the night," croaked Dakin. "Remember Clint Fosdick?"

"Sure. Houschold Fixtures. Slocum near Upper Whistling. What's old Clint done?"

"Got himself murdered last night," mumbled Dakin, "and I can tell you who did it, only I'm not goin' to. I want *you* to tell *me*."

Ellery stared at the author of this extraordinary statement as the car slid across the icy Square and began to creep up Dade Street. "Why? Aren't you sure?"

"I wish I was as sure of a pew in Heaven," cried Chief Dakin. "I'm not only sure who murdered Clint, I know *how* he murdered Clint, and what's more I've got him dead to rights with the evidence to convict."

"Then what's the problem, Dakin?"

"GI," said Wrightsville's chief of police.

"G-what?"

"GI. Those two letters mean anything to you, Mr. Queen?"

"Well, of course—"

"The only trouble is, it don't fit with my evidence," said Dakin. "And if I can't make it fit with my evidence, a smart lawyer might befuddle a jury with it just enough to put a reasonable doubt in their little minds. So you listen to the facts without prejudice, Mr. Queen," the chief said grimly, "and you make that GI fit. Remember the Smith boys—the brothers we've always called the Presidents?"

"Smith? Presidents?" Ellery looked bewildered.

"Their dad was Jeff Smith—Thomas Jefferson Smith, taught American History at Wrightsville High. Jeff married Martha Higgins and they had three sons. Wash, the eldest, was in the war and he's a lawyer now, when he works at it. Linc was in the service, too, then he went to medical school—he's just finishin' his internship at Wrightsville General. And Woodie, the youngest, was drafted into the Army three months back.

"Well, Clint Fosdick was sweet on Martha Higgins since way before she married Jeff Smith. But Clint was eighteen years Martha's senior, he'd never got past fourth grade in school —never even learned to write Spencerian, just printed his letters—and with Jeff, a college man, in the picture Clint didn't stand a chance.

"But in '37 Jeff Smith drowned in Quctonokis Lake while he was counselin' at a boys' summer camp, Martha found herself a penniless widow with three hungry boys to rear, and there was old faithful Clint, still waitin' . . . Well, Martha married him," growled Dakin, "and Clint bought that big house on Hill Drive—the one with those hundred-and-twenty-year-old shade trees—for them all to live in like he was standin' treat for the ice cream at a Sunday School picnic."

And the chief's Adam's apple jiggled as the police car felt for the top of the ridge and began to skid along Hill Drive between the tombs of Wrightsville's fine old mansions.

"Clint did everything for those boys. He sent 'em to college in style. Gave 'em their own cars, pockets full of allowance money . . . When Martha died in the flu epidemic durin' the war, Clint became father *and* mother to them. He couldn't do enough.

"And you'd have said they reciprocated. They called him

Dad. They always remembered his birthday and Father's Day and Christmas. Brought their problems to him—real pal stuff. Young Woodie, the one just went in the Army, ran wild as Ivor Crosby's Ayrshire bull for a while, but Clint kept sayin' he'd spoiled the boy; and it's a fact they were mighty close. Linc—the doctor—he's always been kind of studious and intense; Clint said no man had a finer son. As for Wash, the eldest, he was the easygoin' sort—too easygoin' for this world, Clint used to say; he had to bail Wash out of trouble every other Saturday night, a poker debt or a Low Village girl or somethin', or get him down to his law office on time; but Clint claimed there wasn't a mean bone in Wash's body.

"Well, he was wrong about one of them," said the old police chief, glaring at Ellery, "because one of 'em's poisoned him, and I'll see the murderin' chuck sizzle like pork sausage in a dirty fryin' pan—if you'll tell me what GI means, Mr. Queen!"

"Glad to," said Ellery patiently, "if you'll only explain—"

But they were drawing up before the snow-shrouded Fosdick lawns, and Dakin fell silent. They shook the snow from their overshoes in the stained-glass vestibule, and the police chief led the way through the gloom of the broad entrance hall past one of his young officers to Clint Fosdick's library.

"This is where Clint's housekeeper, Lettie Dowling, found him last night when she heard a chair crash and ran in."

It was a wonderful old high-ceilinged, oak-paneled, darkish room, but Ellery found its present musty silence dispiriting. He saw at once where the body must have been lying—the leather-backed swivel chair behind the desk had fallen over on its side, and the Oriental rug beneath was badly wrinkled, as if it had been clawed in agony.

In a litter of papers on the desk lay an overturned cocktail glass. On a tray nearby stood a pitcher half full of an almost colorless liquid. Ellery stooped over the pitcher, sniffing.

"Yep, he got it in the cocktail," nodded Chief Dakin. "Clint used to be a teetotaler, like me, but when Martha died he developed a hankerin' for martinis. He'd sit here in his library nights when he'd get to feelin' lonely for her, gulpin' 'em down."

"Who mixed this?" asked Ellery sharply.

"That won't tell you anythin'. Clint did it himself. I'll cut some corners for you," said Dakin in a deadly voice. "The housekeeper, old Lettie, has her room just off the kitchen. Yesterday mornin', very early—quarter past six—Lettie, who's got a cold and 'd had a bad night, got out of bed for some aspirin. She heard clinky sounds from the pantry, where the liquor's kept, and she opened her door a crack. There was an almost full bottle of gin that Wash had brought home for Clint Wednesday night, and through the open kitchen door Lettie saw one of the Smith brothers monkeyin' with it. He had a little kind of medicine bottle, she says, in his hand. She saw his face plain.

"Then she heard Clint's voice. Clint was comin' down to the kitchen for his mornin' coffee—earlier than usual, but he knew Lettie was sick. She heard Clint ask the boy what he was doin', and the boy mumbled somethin' and went back upstairs. But Lettie'd seen him put the gin bottle back quick when he'd heard Clint comin' and jam the medicine bottle—empty, she says—in the pocket of his bathrobe. And, Mr. Queen, I've got that 'medicine' bottle. Dug it out of the garbage pit in the back yard late last night where it wouldn't have been if the garbage truck had come yesterday afternoon the way it was scheduled to, only the heavy snow and icy roads held 'em up. That bottle contained poison—if it was full, the way Lettie says it was, there was enough to wipe out half of High Village. And it's the same poison, the Connhaven lab says, that's in the bottle of gin. Besides, *his prints are on the poison bottle.* I've got the devil cold."

"Except, apparently," said Ellery, "for GI. Which is—?"

Chief Dakin carefully removed an uncreased sheet of paper from his overcoat pocket. "Clint was makin' out his monthly store bills when he swallowed that cocktail. He must have known right off he was a goner; it's a quick-actin' poison. And the minute he realized he was poisoned he must have known who'd done it. He probably saw the same thing yesterday mornin' that Lettie saw when he was kitchen-bound for his coffee. It must have puzzled him at the time, but what he'd seen told him the answer in a flash when he felt what he'd swallowed. So before he died Clint got hold of his ballpoint pen and wrote on this letterhead in that schoolboy printin' style of his. Then he fell over with the chair and died on the floor, like a poisoned dog."

"GI?" Ellery reached.

Chief Dakin handed Ellery the paper.

It was an ordinary business billhead. Below the *Clint Fosdick, Household Fixtures, High Village, Terms: 30 Days* inscription appeared in shaky handprinting the two letters:

$$G I$$

"GI," Ellery repeated. "And they've *all* been in the Army, you say?"

"That's right."

"And they were *all* home yesterday morning?"

"Linc's had a few days off from the hospital. Young Woodie's on leave from Camp Hale. Wash lives here all the time."

Ellery was silent, staring at Clint Fosdick's dying message. Then he said, "Does the guilty one know he's tagged for frying?"

"No. Lettie's told nobody but me what she saw, and I haven't let on because of this piece of paper. I've just made out like all three brothers are under suspicion."

"Well," said Ellery. "Could we have the—what did you call them, Dakin?—the Presidents in for a chat?"

The three tall pale young men brought in by their guards were badly in need of sleep and a shave. Their brotherhood was plain from their dark coloring, deep brown eyes, and the way they huddled.

One, a baby-faced variant of the other two in a rumpled U.S. Army uniform, would be Private Woodie Smith. Private Smith's brown eyes masked fear and confusion; his boyish lips quivered.

The second had the keen red-rimmed look of hospitals, and hands so scrubbed they looked bleached—obviously the intern, Dr. Linc Smith. He was gaunt and sharpened down and very quiet. He had been, Ellery would have sworn, crying.

So the third was the lawyer brother Wash—Wash the easygoing, with a heavying gray face and a softened body. Wash Smith stood there weakly smiling, like a professional comedian caught in a tragedy and trying desperately to think of a joke.

"GI," murmured Ellery. "That's what your stepfather wrote down, Private Smith, and what does it suggest to you?"

"What am I supposed to do," whispered the boy in uniform,

"confess because he wrote down GI? I wouldn't kill Dad—why would I kill Dad?"

"Why would Private Smith kill Dad, Dakin?" asked Ellery.

Dakin said coarsely, "Because he might not want to wait for Clint to die natural so he could collect his one-third of Clint's estate that's willed to the three Smith boys."

"Let me alone!" shrieked the boy.

"Woodie," said his brother Linc gently.

"GI," said Ellery. "Comes into your field in a way, Dr. Smith, doesn't it? GI—gastrointestinal?"

The young intern's fatigued eyes widened. "Are you serious? Of course. You can hardly study internal medicine without covering gastroenterology. I even treated Dad Clint for gastrointestinal flu last spring, at his insistence, although if the Medical Board found out . . . And naturally I have access to any amount of poison. The only thing is, I didn't poison him."

"But the GI, Dr. Smith?" Ellery insisted.

The intern shrugged. "If Dad had thought I'd poisoned him, he'd have written my name. That would make sense. GI doesn't. Not to me, anyway."

"Or to me," cried Wash Smith, as if he could not wait.

So Ellery glanced at the lawyer brother. "Gin begins with the letters GI. And it was the bottle of gin that was poisoned, Mr. Smith—a bottle I understand *you* had brought home for Mr. Fosdick."

"Well, sure, he asked me to," said the eldest brother in a sort of agony. "But what kind of way is that to identify somebody? Linc's right. Whoever Clint thought had poisoned him, wouldn't he have written the name?"

Ellery smiled ruefully; he had been chewing on that one for some time. Chief Dakin's face told nothing.

And suddenly Ellery stopped smiling, as if he had recognized the taste in his mouth. "Presidents," he said. "Presidents! Your blood-father, I'm told, gentlemen, was named after President Thomas Jefferson. And he named his three sons after Presidents, too?"

"Why, yes," said Wash Smith blankly. "After the three Presidents he always maintained were the greatest. I was named after Washington."

"After Lincoln," said Dr. Linc Smith.

"After Woodrow Wilson," quavered Private Woodie Smith.

And all three said in one voice, "Why?"

But all Ellery replied was, "Thank you. Would you mind stepping out of the room?" It was only when their guards had herded the three Smiths out that Ellery said to Dakin, "Now I can tell you whom old Clint was accusing of murder."

"I'm listening," said Chief Dakin.

Ellery was looking at the fallen chair as if the old man who had toppled it were still with them, gripping a pen and trying to push it along a billhead.

"Because Dr. Smith is right," Ellery said. "Fancy verbal acrobatics are the pleasant preoccupations of detective fiction. In real life they don't happen. A man who will perform the miracle of forcing his dying brain and muscles to commit a message to paper is not trying to be subtle or clever. If he knows who did the job on him his efforts can have only one purpose: to transmit that information as directly as he can. Clint Fosdick, in writing those two letters, GI, was trying to do just one thing: *Name his killer.*"

But Dakin's expression did not change. "GI isn't even a part of any of their names, Mr. Queen. Don't you think I thought of that?"

"Well, Clint did have a problem, Dakin. Suppose the poisoner had been Wash Smith. Clint must have realized that he might start to write down the name Wash, or Washington, *but never get beyond the first letter*—he knew he was going fast. But if all he could manage to write down were the W of Washington, that W would apply equally to young Woodie, named after President Wilson. So, to avoid being misunderstood, Clint simply began to print his poisoner's *first* name."

"First name?" The police chief blinked.

"Thomas Jefferson Smith named his three sons after Presidents. So the boys' full names, like Jeff Smith's own, must begin with the first names of the Presidents they were named for. In fact, Private Smith is actually called Woodie, obviously for Woodrow Wilson Smith. Dr. Linc Smith's full name, then, must be Abraham Lincoln Smith. A for Abraham (or L for Lincoln), W for Woodrow (or for Wilson)—neither fits the GI.

"But how about Wash-for-Washington Smith," said Ellery, "always having to be bailed out of trouble, a lawyer 'when he works at it'—probably over his ears in debt and desperately needing his third of Clint's fortune now? There's your chuck in the woodpile, Dakin—the brother Lettie Dowling saw dosing the gin bottle with poison in the pantry yesterday morning. It was George Washington Smith Lettie saw, wasn't it? It's his fingerprints on the poison bottle?"

"Yes," said Wrightsville's chief of police slowly. "Wash is my man, all right. But Mr. Queen, Clint wrote GI—and Wash's first name, George, starts with GE."

"Tricky," said Ellery, squeezing Dakin's arm. "Poor old Clint got the G down all right, Dakin, but he died just as he completed the downstroke of the E."

NARCOTICS DEPT.

The Black Ledger

THE CASE OF THE BLACK LEDGER WAS one of the biggest cases Ellery ever undertook, and its size was not reduced by the littleness of the effort involved. It consisted merely in acting as an errand boy, the errand being to take the ledger from the City of New York to Washington, D.C.

Why the transportation from one city to another of an account book worth perhaps three dollars should be a problem, why Ellery was the messenger instead of a federal agent, why he deliberately set forth on his mission alone, without even a weapon . . . the answers to these engrossing questions may be found in the proper place, which is not here. This story begins where that one ends.

In appearance the Black Ledger was unexciting. It had a hard binding lined with black leatherette which was scraped along the edges; its dimensions were six inches by eight and one-half inches, and it contained fifty-two thick, limp ledger pages rule-printed in blue and red lines, and all rather dirty. And yet it was one of the most infamous and historic volumes in the library of American crime. For on the blue lines of those fifty-two jammed pages were written the name and address of every important regional distributor of illegal narcotics in the United States, and the list was in the handwriting of the master of the ring.

In the spreading epidemic of dope addiction which was plaguing the forty-eight states, the federal authorities wanted this list desperately. The Black Ledger was a monstrous indiscretion, and to keep it from reaching Washington the quiet monster who had compiled it would stop at literally nothing. The two government agents who secured possession of it paid for their triumph with their lives. But by that time the Black Ledger was—for the moment—safe in New York.

At this point Ellery entered the problem.

The place where he examined the ledger and accepted the mission and prepared to carry it out was, they were positive, under surveillance. The chieftain of this continent-wide criminal organization was no petty gang lord. He was a genius of withered soul, with immense power, resources, and connections, who had raised vicious crime almost to the level of respectable big business. Ordinary methods were bound to fail. At the least, a show of force on the spot might turn the entire area into a bloody battlefield, causing the deaths of innocent people. Ellery's plan was accepted.

A drawing room on the Capitol Limited was reserved for him officially by telephone, and at the appointed time Ellery went down into the streets.

The fall day was gray, with raw skies, and Ellery had hung an umbrella with a bamboo handle over his left arm. He was wearing a lined topcoat and he carried a bulging briefcase.

Ellery seemed unaware that from the instant his foot touched the pavement his life expectancy dwindled to the vanishing point. Smoking his big brier pipe placidly, he stepped to the curb and glanced around as if for a taxicab.

Two things happened at once. His arms were seized from behind and a seven-passenger sedan shot to the curb and blocked him off.

The next moment he was in the car, prisoner of four large men whose complete silence was more quieting than threats.

Ellery was not surprised when the sedan deposited them at Pennsylvania Station and three of his four silent captors strolled him unarguably through Gate 3 down into the Capitol Limited and Drawing Room A of the fifth car, which was his reservation. Two of the large men took him in and one of them carefully bolted the drawing room door.

As Ellery had expected, the monster was waiting for him. He occupied the best armchair, an immaculately dressed man of middle age with grudging pale hair parted cleverly in the middle and hot, sore-looking eyes. This creature was a millionaire, thought Ellery, a millionaire who had made his millions by destroying the will and health and future of thousands of foolish people, many of them children and adolescents.

And Ellery said, "You had the phone tapped, of course."

The narcotics king did not reply. He glanced at the larger of his two strong-arm men, the one with the boneless nose.

Nose said instantly, "He didn't speak to nobody when he come out. Nobody come near him. He didn't touch nothing. He didn't drop nothing."

The monster in the chair glanced at the other large man, the one with the tic in his right eyelid.

"Nobody else gets out up there," said Tic. "And Al is keeping in touch by the train phone from the lounge."

The sore eyes now turned their full animal suffering on Ellery. "You want to live?" He had a soft, womanish voice.

"As much as the next man," said Ellery, trying to keep his tongue from rattling.

"Then hand it over."

Ellery swallowed and said, "Oh, come."

Nose grinned, but the monster said to him, "No. First open his bag."

Nose dumped the contents of Ellery's briefcase on the floor. It consisted of a single object, a crisp new Manhattan telephone directory.

"Nothing else in the bag?"

"Not a thing." Nose tossed the empty briefcase to one side. He picked up the big directory and riffled it twice.

"Screwy thing to be lugging around," remarked Tic.

"My favorite train reading," said Ellery. He felt urgently like asking for a drink of water, but he decided against it.

"Not in here," said Nose.

"His coat and hat."

Nose shucked him like an ear of corn while Tic examined Ellery's snapbrim.

"It wouldn't be in here," he complained. "It's too big."

Nose jeered. "With the cover it's too big. This is a smart operator. He tore out the pages and crumbled 'em."

"But fifty-two pages," protested Tic.

The monster said nothing. His red glance was fixed on the furled umbrella, which Ellery had retrieved and was clutching. Suddenly he reached over and yanked. He removed the umbrella cover slowly and slowly pressed the catch and pushed. The umbrella opened. After a moment he tossed it away.

Nose said, "Not in the coat." The lining lay on the floor, he had torn the pockets out, and he had ripped the seams wherever the material doubled over.

"Strip him."

Ellery felt his knees buckle under the pain of Nose's grip. Tic did the stripping, without kindness. Sore Eyes watched the denuding process with the unblinking patience of a crocodile.

"Leave me my shorts!" said Ellery wildly.

They left him nothing. Mother-naked, he was permitted to wrap himself in the wreck of his topcoat, crouch in a chair, and smoke his pipe. It tasted like fuming brass, but it gave him comfort.

He reached for the Manhattan telephone book just as the Capitol Limited pulled out of Pennsylvania Station. He knew that the conductor was taken care of and that there would be no interruptions until he reached Washington—if indeed he ever reached it.

But he was wrong. At Newark, when the train stopped, a man entered the drawing room. Nose called him Doc. Doc, a fat little man with three chins and no hair, was carrying a black bag. He eyed Ellery with the brisk anticipation of a professor approaching the cadaver tank in a dissecting room.

Ellery clutched the Manhattan directory and braced himself.

The Limited was roaring through New Brunswick when Doc, busily at work, referred to himself jestingly as Secretary of the Interior. By the time the train was rolling into the Trenton station Doc was no longer jesting: he was perspiring.

Shutting his bag, he made his report to the man in the armchair in a strained voice.

It was negative.

The man in the armchair said to Tic, "Tell Al to phone Philly. I want Jig with some equipment." Then he looked at Ellery and for the first time showed his false teeth in a nightmarish smile. "Secret writing," he said softly. "Just in case."

Jig got on at North Philadelphia. At Wilmington Nose made some exterior reports, and Jig completed them. Jig was a tall skinny man with no shoulders and a club foot.

The Black Ledger, whole or in parts, was not in Ellery's suit, as the ruins of his trousers and jacket testified. His oxford shirt, necktie, undershirt, shorts, and socks had been carefully manhandled. His shoes had been tapped, probed, slit, and all but turned inside out. Even his belt, an unmistakably single strip of cowhide, had been cut apart.

All his possessions were on display. Keys and coins were pronounced solid. His wallet contained ninety-seven dollars, a money order stub, a New York State operator's license, a dues receipt from the Mystery Writers of America, five business cards, and seven jottings of ideas for stories. His checkbook had been gone over page by page, including the stubs. His tobacco pouch had been found to contain pipe tobacco, and an unopened packet of cigarets was opened and found to contain cigaret tobacco. A letter from his publisher demanded the return of galley proofs three weeks overdue, and a letter postmarked Orangeburg, New York, from a man signing himself Joseph MacCurty threatened to kill Ellery Queen unless Ellery Queen saved the writer from being killed by an invisible enemy.

And Jig caressed his Adam's apple and said that nothing from, on, or about the guy concealed secret writing. This covered every surface capable of taking a fluid impression, not excluding the guy's epidermis. Jig used the word epidermis.

By this time they were approaching Elkton, Maryland.

The monster sucked his lower lip in silence.

"Maybe," said Nose in the silence, "maybe he memorized the names . . . huh?"

"Yeah!" Tic looked relieved. "They could still have the book back in New York and he's carrying it all in his head."

The man in the chair looked up. "There's twenty-eight names to a page, and fifty-two pages—almost fifteen hundred names. Who is he, Einstein?" He said suddenly: "That phone book you picked up again. What's the gag?"

Ellery tamped a fresh load into his pipe to give his fingers something to do. "Some people relax with mystery stories. I can't—I write them. The phone book does it for me."

"I bet." The sore eyes glittered. "Jig, give that book the business!"

Nose tore it from Ellery's hand.

"But I already tested it for secret writing," said Jig.

"To hell with secret writing. We're after a list of names. And in a New York phone book you got about every kind of name there is! Look for marks next to names—pinpricks, pencil dots, impressions of nails—anything!"

"Would someone mind," Ellery asked plaintively, "giving me a light?"

They were pulling into Washington when Jig came back from the compartment in which he had set up his impromptu laboratory.

"No marks," he mumbled. "No nothing. It's just the way it came off the press."

"And nobody's still tried to leave that joint in New York we got covered," muttered Tic. "Al phoned from Baltimore."

The man in the chair said slowly, "So he's a decoy after all. They figured they'd pull us off with him while some other —— got away. Only they got another figure coming. Sooner or later the real boy scout's got to try to sneak out of that building. Tic, get Al to phone New York and tell Manno if anybody gets away he can start cutting his throat . . . Okay, you." He looked at Ellery. "You can get dressed now."

The Capitol Limited was standing in the Washington terminal when Ellery, looking more like a hobo after a bad season than a respectable gentleman-writer-detective, picked up his umbrella and said with pale whimsicality, "Do I get shot in the back as I leave, or are all bets off?"

"Wait a minute," said the monster.

"Yes?" said Ellery, nervously gripping his umbrella.

"Where you going with the umbrella?"

"Umbrella?" Ellery glanced blankly down at it. "Why, you examincd this yourself—"

"So that was it," and now the womanish voice had a vicious sting. "I examined it, all right—the wrong part! *It's in the bamboo handle.* You rolled up the pages of the ledger and stuffed them into the hollow head of that bumbershoot! Take it from him!"

Ellery found himself in Tic's grip staring fascinated as Nose demolished the handle of the umbrella.

And when it was thoroughly demolished there was nothing on the floor of the drawing room but some curved splinters of bamboo.

The monster rose, his sore eyes smoldering. "Boot him," he choked, "boot him out of here!"

Twenty-six minutes later Ellery was escorted into the private office of a very important executive of a very important branch of the government in a very important building in Washington.

"I'm the messenger from New York," said Ellery, "and I've brought you the Black Ledger."

Ellery did not see the monster again until the trial in federal court. They met in the corridor during a recess. The narcotics king was surrounded by bailiffs and lawyers and newspapermen, and he was looking exactly like a criminal who expects the worst. Nevertheless, the moment he spied Ellery his face brightened and he jumped forward and seized Ellery by the arm and pulled him aside.

"Keep those monkeys away from here a minute!" he shouted, and then he said piteously: "Queen, you're a lifesaver. This thing's been driving me bats. Ever since you outsmarted me on that damn train, I've been asking myself how you did it. It wasn't on you, it wasn't in you, it wasn't in that phone book or umbrella. So where was it? Would you please tell me?"

"I don't mind kicking a man when he's down," said Ellery coldly, "not when he's a so-called man like you. Certainly I'll tell you. The phone book and umbrella were herrings. I had to keep you occupied with your own royal cleverness. The ledger never left my hand."

"What are you giving me?" howled the monster.

"It's the size of the ledger and the quantity of its contents that threw you. You never stopped to think that size and quantity can be reduced."

"Huh?"

"Microfilm," said Ellery. "During the war the government used it to reduce each letter of troop mail to one quarter of a square inch. A ton of ordinary mail—eighty-five thousand letters—on microfilm weighs only twenty pounds. All I had to do was have fifty-two sheets six by eight and a half inches photographed down to microfilm. Result: a mere thirteen feet of film less than a half-inch in width. When it was wound up in a tight roll . . ."

"But in your *hand*," said the monster dazedly. "I'd have bet a million to one you couldn't be palming anything . . ."

"I'd hardly have taken a foolish chance like that," said Ellery. "No, the roll of film was in something—in fact, in two things. And I kept applying matches to it regularly all the way from New York to Washington."

"Matches! You set *fire* to it?"

"Nice touch, don't you think? Oh, it was in a fireproof container, an old cartridge shell just big enough to hold it, and capped tightly. The container was tucked away in the bottom of my pipe bowl—the only thing I carried you didn't search. It made a brassy smoke," said Ellery, "but when I think of all those kids who've learned to smoke your marijuana and shoot themselves full of your heroin, I'd say it was worth it—wouldn't you?"

KIDNAPING DEPT.

Child Missing!

THE BILLY HARPER kidnaping case—in Sergeant Thomas Velie's quaint linguistic goulash—took the cake for kicking the form sheet in the brisket. For one thing—and there were others —the FBI came into it at no time whatsoever. Inspector Queen explained the abstention of the Federal Bureau by saying that he could hardly bother J. Edgar's Ph.D.s with a crime problem that never amounted to more than child's play.

But the Inspector said that after Ellery solved the case. At the time it did not seem a simple business at all.

Billy Harper was only seven years old—a bright but unfortunate child, everyone agreed. When you were seven, it was an unhappy experience to be taken away from your father's big house beside the park and to be installed in a little box of a hotel apartment across town with your swollen-nosed mother and a nurse who was pretty but hardly a substitute for your father.

Billy had heard bitter words like "divorce" and "No-I-won't-give-up-ten-years-of-my-life-quite-*that*-easily-Lloyd-Harper!" Also, some mysterious creature named "Jarryl Jones" had been booted about in the parental war which Billy had illegally heard raging from abovestairs that dreadful night. (This Jarryl Jones was a "model," it seemed, which made no sense at all, since models were airplanes and ships and things.) An unknown word, "infatuation," came into it several times, and a vaguely frightening one called "custody" which got both his parents very angry indeed. And finally Billy's mother said something icy-sharp about "a six months' trial separation," whatever that was, "after which, if you still think you want to marry this girl, Lloyd, I'll give you your divorce." And then his mother and Miss M'Govern had taken Billy away to the little box on the other side of the park, leaving his father behind. When Miss M'Govern took Billy to visit his father, which she did every Friday afternoon thereafter, the greatest man in the world was so tightly gentle it scared Billy, because that wasn't his father at all—in the old days he had bellowed and roughhoused wonderfully. It was like visiting a stranger. And as Billy roamed disconsolately over his old house from cellar to attic on those Friday afternoons, the house was a stranger, too. Whatever it meant, it was devastating.

And then Billy Harper was kidnaped.

He was snatched at a few minutes past 6 P.M. after the fifth consecutive Friday visit to his father's house. Miss M'Govern sobbed that she had turned her back on Billy for no more than a *second*—to post a letter at the West Side exit from the park on their way back from Mr. Harper's—but when she looked around Billy had disappeared.

At first Miss M'Govern had been annoyed, thinking he had darted back into the park against her strict injunction. But when she could not find him she became alarmed and sought a policeman. The policeman had no better luck. Calls from the park station to Mrs. Harper's apartment and Lloyd Harper's house brought Billy's parents on the run; each said that Billy had not come "home," and they quarreled over the sad ambiguous word while the desk sergeant tried patiently to get it all straight. With night coming on the entire park patrol was alerted for "a lost boy seven years of age"; by 3 A.M. the last negative report was in, it dawned on everyone that Billy's disappearance might have a grimmer explanation, and a general alarm went out.

Lloyd Harper was a wealthy man; the Harpers had been mentioned slyly in several recent newspaper columns; one columnist had stacked his story by referring to young Billy's Friday afternoon "commutation trips across the park."

It began to add up.

Inspector Queen of headquarters entered the case at 8 o'clock the following morning. At 9:06 A.M. the postman on his regular rounds delivered Lloyd Harper's mail; at 9:12 A.M. Inspector Queen made a certain surreptitious telephone call; at 9:38 A.M. Ellery rang the Harper bell and was admitted by none other than Sergeant Velie of the Inspector's staff.

"This," the Sergeant announced to Ellery forbiddingly, "is one for the nanny goats."

Ellery found his father in the drawing room making like a spectator. The little Inspector came to him at once.

"The FBI? No, not yet, son," said the Inspector in an affable *sotto voce*. "It's kind of a funny case. . . . Yes, there's been a ransom note, but wait till Piggott's through with that nurse. . . . Who? Oh, the babe who's sitting there doing a burn. That's Jarryl Jones, the other woman. Harper had a date with her last night which of course he couldn't keep, and she stormed over first thing this morning to give him what-for and walked into this. Bet she's sorry, heh-heh! Shhh." Jarryl Jones was beautiful and Mibs Harper—at least this morning—was definitely not; nevertheless, Lloyd Harper stood over his wife's chair, stubble-cheeked and hollow-eyed, with his back to his great love.

Miss M'Govern talked breathily. No, she had nothing to hide. The letter which she had turned her back on little Billy Harper to post the day before? It had been addressed to her boy friend. Mr. Harper will tell you. Ralph Kleinschmidt is his name. Ralph Kleinschmidt had been the Harpers' chauffeur . . . sort of a hothead, yes . . . he did drink a bit too much at times . . .

"I fired him two weeks ago for drunkenness," said Lloyd Harper shortly. "With no references. He got pretty nasty."

"Lloyd! Do you really think—?"

"So he's getting even," said Velie sadly. "Now you don't want to get mixed up in this, girlie, so what's the address you wrote on your letter to this guy?"

"General Delivery, main post office," whispered Miss M'Govern. "We've corresponded that way before when one of us was on the wing looking for a job—"

"Where's Kleinschmidt's hideout?" barked Detective Piggott.

"I don't know! Won't you believe me? Anyway, Ralph wouldn't—couldn't do a thing like this. . . ."

At Inspector Queen's unexcited nod, Piggott took her down to headquarters.

"We're wasting valuable time," snarled Lloyd Harper.

"I want my baby," moaned Mibs Harper.

"That ransom note, Inspector—!"

"Yes, the ransom note," said Inspector Queen, producing an envelope. "Ellery, what do you make of this?"

The envelope was squarish and large, of heavy cream-colored crushed bond. Obviously expensive. Lloyd Harper's address was blocklettered in smeary pencil in a style so crude as almost to defy deciphering. The envelope had passed through the local substation the night before; from the postmark, about two hours after Billy Harper's abduction.

The single sheet of notepaper inside was made to fit a much smaller envelope. It was tinted mauve, a fine deckle-edged rag paper.

The same smeary, crude blockprinting said, without salutation: *The price is 50 grand to get the kid back safe. Small bills in oilcloth bundle. Father to drive alone by southwest corner La Brea and Wilshire Boulevards, exactly 11:15 a.m. today, throw bundle to sidewalk, keep going. Follow orders or else.* There was no signature.

"Mailed last night, couldn't possibly be delivered before this morning's mail," said Inspector Queen, "which was a few minutes past nine. . . ."

"I take it what you have in mind," murmured Ellery, "is

that, the southwest corner of La Brea and Wilshire Boulevards being located in only one city in the world—Los Angeles, California—and the time for deposit of the ransom money on said corner being set for 11:15 this morning, the whole thing's impossible."

"Which the kidnaper of course knows," said the Inspector. "It'll be a long time before you can go from Manhattan to Los Angeles in two hours. So you agree, Ellery, this note is a phony?"

"I agree," said Ellery, frowning at the note, "that something is awfully wrong. . . ."

"I want action!" shouted Billy's father.

"You, Mr. Harper, want a kick in the pants," said Inspector Queen unexpectedly. "I've been sniffing your premises." He took from his pocket a handful of large, squarish white envelopes. "Identical with the envelope the note came in. Your envelope, Mr. Harper. *You didn't snatch your own boy to get him away from his ma, now, did you?* And use the note as a red herring?"

Billy's father sank into a chair. "Mibs, I swear to you—!"

"Where's Billy?" screamed his wife. "What did you do with my child, you—you baby-snatcher!"

"Oh, come off it, Mrs. H," said a voice, and they all looked around to see the beautiful Miss Jones uncrossing her famous legs and rising to her much photographed height. "Take a look at that notepaper, Inspector. It's hers."

"Mrs. Harper's?" said Ellery, elevating his brows.

"That's right. She wrote me a threatening letter on paper just like it only last week." Jarryl Jones laughed. "She's stashed the kid somewhere and sent the note, using one of Lloyd's envelopes to frame him for the foul deed. A woman scorned, et cetera. Darlin', you owe me a meal from last night. How about brunch?"

But Lloyd Harper was staring at his wife.

She said slowly, "Of course it isn't true. I wouldn't do a thing like that, Lloyd. And if I did, I wouldn't be so stupid as to use my own notepaper."

"Or me to use my own envelopes, Mibs," groaned Harper. "Anybody could have got hold of one of my envelopes, Inspector Queen—or for that matter of a sheet of my wife's stationery. Somebody's framing me—her—us!"

The Inspector patted his mustache agitatedly. Then he muttered, "Time," and took Ellery aside. "Son . . ."

"Let's wait," Ellery soothed him. "Till the Sergeant gets back."

"Velie? Where'd he go, Ellery?"

"I sent him over to our apartment to get something out of my newspaper file. I want to check my memory."

"Of *what?*"

"Of a feature story I read a couple of Sundays ago, Dad. If I'm right, it's going to clear this thing up."

Sergeant Velie reappeared twenty minutes later, just after Inspector Queen received two reports—one that the nurse, Miss M'Govern, had not yet revealed the whereabouts of Ralph Kleinschmidt, the other that the all-night city-wide search for little Billy Harper had failed to turn up a trace of him. Mrs. Harper was weeping again, the beautiful Miss Jones was telling Mr. Harper off, and Mr. Harper was glaring at the beautiful Miss Jones with homicide in his bloodshot eyes.

"Thank you, Sergeant!" Ellery snatched the gaudy Sunday supplement and turned to the center spread. "Ah. . . . See this?" He flourished the newspaper. "It's the story of a kidnaping in California a year or so ago. The child was recovered when the FBI caught the kidnaper, and the man was tried under the Lindbergh law and found guilty. He was executed a few weeks ago, which is why the story was rehashed in this Sunday feature. Now let me read you the original ransom note sent by the California kidnaper to the father of the kidnaped California child." And Ellery read, "*The price is 50 grand to get the kid back safe. Small bills in oilcloth bundle. Father to drive alone by southwest corner La Brea and Wilshire Boulevards, exactly 11:15 a.m. today . . .*"

"The same note," gasped Inspector Queen.

"Identical, Dad. Right down to the *Follow orders or else.* And that tells us," said Ellery, whirling, "who's behind the snatch of Billy Harper."

And everyone was still as Billy's space helmet on his father's bust of George Washington.

"The kidnaper of Billy Harper," Ellery went on, waving the supplement, "not only used the ransom note in the year-old California case as the model for *his* ransom note, he even duplicated the Los Angeles street corner indicated in the California note as the place for the payment of the Harper money. That is, the kidnaper appointed an *impossible* meeting place! Why should he have done this? If the kidnaping of Billy were a blind—if, let us say, Mr. Harper wanted to take possession of his little boy and make it seem to everyone, especially his wife, like an outside abduction for the usual ransom—he would hardly have designated an impossible place for the 'payment' of the ransom, making the whole business suspect at once, when all he had to do was name a rendezvous in the New York area and simply fail to have his mythical 'kidnaper' show up.

The criminal would be thought to have changed his mind or been scared off.

"So the designation of Los Angeles as the payoff place in the Harper case makes utterly no sense—that is," said Ellery softly, "if you think of the kidnaper as someone with the capacity to realize how impossible it is. But suppose the writer of the Harper note *didn't* realize that New York and Los Angeles are three thousand miles apart?"

"Why, Maestro," said Sergeant Velie, "a moron knows that."

"An adult moron, perhaps, Sergeant," said Ellery with a smile. "But even a bright little boy of seven may be excused for his ignorance. Mr. and Mrs. Harper, I'm happy to say that your son Billy was kidnaped by none other than—himself! This Sunday supplement story probably gave him the idea, and in his enthusiasm he copied the California ransom note word for word. He used a sheet of your notepaper, Mrs. Harper, and one of your envelopes, Mr. Harper, not realizing that in doing so he was implicating both his mommy and his daddy. . . . Where is he?" Ellery grinned in answer to Billy Harper's father's rather grim question. "Well, my hunch is—based on this and that—that Billy went back across the park last evening, after giving Miss M'Govern the slip, and sneaked into this very house, Mr. Harper. . . ."

They found young Billy holed up behind an old trunk in the attic surrounded by the crusts of six cream cheese and jelly sandwiches, two empty milk bottles, and thirteen comic books —definitely awed, Sergeant Velie counted them. Billy said he had snatched himself 'cause it seemed like an excitin' thing to do. But Ellery has always held the young man to be a psychological prodigy who knew just what to do to make two rather difficult adults patch up his personal world again. There is no way of proving this, but it is significant that Miss Jarryl Jones was seen with Lloyd Parker no more and Mrs. Harper moved right back across the park.